Another *boom* rocked the boat. *The raiders must have water canons*, Spader realized. Only water missiles could do such serious damage.

The speakers crackled, and Spader heard a crash as something toppled to the deck.

He crawled to the instrument panel. The raiders probably figured they had taken out the pilot and navigator since the ship wasn't moving. They didn't know that there was one more person still in the tower— and Spader intended to keep it that way.

He pushed out of his mind the sounds of splashes and the exchange of water bullets, screams, and shouts. He had to stay focused. He didn't know the panel well enough to work it blind from the floor, so he pulled himself up into a crouch, keeping his head low.

He peered over the board. Several skimmers and a life raft bobbed on the water, making good speed. One of the jobs of the aquaneers was to ensure the safety of the passengers. Spader figured the personnel from Crasker were in the raft, with aquaneers on the skimmers guiding them. The rest of the crew would defend the ship.

It was up to him to get them out of there.

PENDRAGON

BEFORE THE WAR

Book One of the Travelers

Coming Soon:

Book Two of the Travelers

Book Three of the Travelers

PENDRAGON
BEFORE THE WAR

BOOK ONE OF THE TRAVELERS

CREATED BY
D. J. MacHale
WRITTEN BY CARLA JABLONSKI

Aladdin Paperbacks
New York   London   Toronto   Sydney

ALADDIN PAPERBACKS
An imprint of Simon & Schuster
Children's Publishing Division
1230 Avenue of the Americas, New York, NY 10020
Copyright © 2009 by D. J. MacHale
All rights reserved, including the right of reproduction
in whole or in part in any form.
ALADDIN PAPERBACKS and related logo are registered
trademarks of Simon & Schuster, Inc.
Designed by Mike Rosamilia
The text of this book was set in Apollo MT.
Manufactured in the United States of America
First Aladdin Paperbacks edition January 2009
2 4 6 8 10 9 7 5 3 1
Library of Congress Control Number 2008929798
ISBN-13: 978-1-4169-6522-0
ISBN-10: 1-4169-6522-X

Contents

BOOK ONE OF THE TRAVELERS

KASHA

ONE

Kasha smelled it before she saw it.

A tang.

Kasha's ears flattened against her head, and her mouth curled back in a silent snarl. She hated tangs. She had good reason: The vicious lizardlike creatures had killed her mother several years ago. Tangs threatened Kasha and the other klees' lives whenever they left the city of Leeandra or ventured off the sky bridges and took to the jungle floor. Tangs were the reason klees built their cities on bridges and platforms in the enormous trees, high above the ground. She and her forage group risked a run-in with tangs every time they worked. Like today.

Now there was one nearby.

She dropped down to all fours and held still, her whiskers twitching. Although she usually stood on her hind legs, Kasha preferred hunkering down low to the ground to assess a situation. And she moved much faster using all four paws.

Tangs were tall, at least seven feet—but the fruit stalks

were taller. All Kasha could see was the occasional flash of its bright green scaly tail thumping the ground.

The tang was holding still too. Kasha hoped that was because the tang hadn't detected her presence. The green stalks didn't camouflage her blue-black fur and dark tunic very well. But the whiff she'd gotten was the usual unpleasant tang stink, not the stench the two-legged monstrosities emitted when going after prey. Kasha intended to keep it that way.

Kasha swiftly slunk through the towering stalks, taking care not to disturb them. Any rustling or movement would be certain to attract the tang's attention. She needed to get back to Boon and Durgen and warn them.

There were two forage groups out today, and the carts were positioned at opposite ends of the harvest area. Pale, furless gars were picking fruit between the two carts and radiating out from them. Gars were stationed with the carts as well, to receive the bags of fruit—and as first fodder for tangs if an attack took place.

Kasha had offered to check the northern plants to see if it would be worth including them in today's forage. The weather had been difficult this growing season, and the fields were ripening at different rates. She'd refused to bring any gars with her for this part of the forage—they were too clumsy and dim-witted, and she feared they'd attract tangs with their noisy movements.

Durgen had protested and suggested they wait until the next flyover to make the determination about harvesting from the air, but Kasha had insisted. The last two forages had been disappointing. She felt it was her responsibility as a forager to ensure an adequate food supply. The entire population of Leeandra depended on the foragers.

Now she wished she hadn't refused the escort.

How many tangs were there? Was this one monstrous creature out on its own, or was it an advance scout searching for food? Food like gars and klees.

She reached the outskirts of the picking area, and as far as she could tell, the tang hadn't followed her. She might be able to get the gars to pack up their sacks and move on without having to face an attack.

Like the tangs, gars were two-legged creatures, but they were much smaller, much weaker. Gars were also smaller and less powerful than the klees; Kasha wasn't sure if that was due to their living conditions or was just the way of their species. It didn't matter really. Gars were what they were.

None of the gars glanced her way as they kept their heads down and their feeble minds on their work. That was good—she didn't want to start a panic. She wanted to get as much of the fruit packed as she could.

Should they bring the cart closer to the gars, or get the gars moving faster toward the cart? In either case, she had to alert the other klees. If there was one tang, there might be more.

Kasha picked up her pace but resisted the urge to break into a full-out run. Her paws padded over the rough ground as she made swift and steady progress toward the cart.

She'd reached a cleared area. A stream of gars was bringing bulging sacks and loading them into the cart. Kasha's friend, Boon, sat in the driver's seat, keeping watch. Durgen, the forage group leader, was supervising the gars. The rest of the klees had gone into the fields with the gars to oversee the work.

Kasha's fur bristled. She heard a rustling behind her. Her nose twitched, picking up the tang's scent.

It was approaching. Time to run.

Her paws hit the ground hard, and she knew she was making more sound than she should, but she had to get to the cart before the tang noticed it.

She raced to the cart—and didn't have to say a word.

"Which direction?" Durgen asked the moment he saw her.

"North," Kasha panted, catching her breath.

"Then we go south!" Boon said, taking up the reins as Kasha leaped up onto the cart. The two zenzens pulling the cart stopped munching on dry grasses and lifted their large orange heads.

"Yah!" Boon shouted, flicking the reins. The zenzens responded with a quick trot, the extra joints in their legs helping them pick up speed quickly.

As soon as the nearby gars saw the cart move, they dropped their sacks and raced after it. They knew all too well what this kind of sudden movement meant.

"Hang on!" Boon exclaimed. He yanked the reins hard, forcing the zenzens into a sharp turn. Kasha slid across the cart while Durgen lunged for the bags of fruit, keeping them from falling out.

Kasha's bones jarred as the cart landed with a jerk, then lurched forward.

"Sorry!" Boon called. He flicked the reins again and urged the zenzens to pick up their pace.

Kasha leaped up to stand, planting her feet wide to keep her balance, her keen eyes searching. "The tang! It spotted us!"

The horrible creature burst out of the stalks. It stood at the edge of the cleared area, its angry red eyes flashing in its reptilian head, and its long green hair tangled into the quivering stalks. Its green tongue flicked out as it hissed, revealing its multiple rows of teeth. Terrified gars scattered in all directions, desperate to escape.

"Go! Go! Go!" Kasha cried.

"I'm going!" Boon shouted back.

The tang's head whipped back and forth. Kasha knew it was trying to decide who to take down. The gars were confusing it by running in so many directions. *Of course,* Kasha thought, *none of them has any idea if there are more tangs out there.* They might only be safe for a moment.

"We're crushing the fields!" Kasha growled in frustration. She hated seeing all those dropped sacks and trampled stalks.

"We're staying alive," Durgen snapped.

The tang made its decision. Kasha turned away as it leaped onto a nearby gar. The gar's agonized howl of pain made the zenzens pick up their pace. The cart rattled and shook, mowing down more stalks as it hurtled across the field.

"How are we doing?" Boon called back.

Kasha turned to look again. "The tang has a gar to keep it busy. That should give us enough time to get away. But we lost so much harvest!"

Kasha suddenly had an idea. She leaped from the moving cart, landing on all fours.

"What are you doing?" Durgen shouted at her. "Get back here!"

Kasha ignored him. She let out a roar to stop the fleeing gars. "Pick up those sacks now!"

"We are not waiting for you!" Durgen was standing in the cart, shouting after her.

"We'll catch up!" Kasha shouted back.

She reached down and grabbed a sack and shoved it into a nearby gar's chest. Startled, he took it from her. "Pick them up! And run!"

The gars did what they were told, as always. The tang was feeding and wouldn't stop until it had finished. That bought them a little time.

Despite what Durgen had said, the cart slowed down. The gars ran to it and hurled in their sacks, then continued running. Kasha brought up the rear and threw in a sack herself before clambering back up.

"That was a very foolish thing to do," Durgen scolded.

Kasha smirked. "But you're glad I did it. We saved a good portion of that forage."

"You take too many chances," Durgen said.

"It was a calculated risk. For the good of Leeandra."

"What do I do?" Boon asked, slowing the zenzen to a wary walk. "Do we stop here and continue to harvest, or do we warn Flor's group?"

"That tang back there may still follow us," Kasha said. "We should probably—"

She stopped speaking when she saw a horde of frantic gars running toward them. From the opposite direction.

"Trouble," Boon growled.

"If they're running this way that must mean . . ."

Durgen nodded grimly. "Tangs. On the other side of the fields."

"So we have at least one tang behind us," Boon said, "and more in front of us."

Kasha hissed in fury. "They're not smart enough to have trapped us. It's a fluke that we're being boxed in."

"Flor's group is in trouble," Durgen said.

"So are we!" Boon cried. The new group of gars joined the others and swarmed the cart, trying to climb in, spooking the zenzens. One of the animals reared, pulling the cart up with it. The sudden movement knocked Kasha off balance. She slammed into the side of the cart, the wind knocked out of her.

Durgen unsheathed his claws and slashed the pale, furless hands reaching into the cart. "Stay back!" he shouted. "Get to the main road! Go!"

"Get away!" Boon cried. "Get away from the zenzens! You'll be crushed!"

Kasha pulled herself upright. Some of the gars listened to the orders and raced away. Others were either too frightened or too stupid to pay attention. They kept trying to get into the cart, but it was moving too quickly.

"We have to get to Flor," Kasha said. "Those klees will need our help!"

"Up ahead!" Boon shouted.

Kasha saw a red-and-brown-striped klee standing in a cart. Flor. He was fending off two tangs. Two dead klees and five dead gars lay on the ground.

Boon pulled the cart to a stop. "How close should we get?"

"Two against one is no match," Kasha said. "Not with tangs."

Durgen pulled a flying disc from his pouch and grabbed a spear that hung on the side of the cart. He stood and aimed. "I can't get a shot from here without hitting Flor," he said, his fur bristling in frustration.

The terrible odor of hungry tangs filled the air. Gars were scattering, running everywhere. The chaos gave Kasha an idea.

"We have to attract the tangs' attention," Kasha said. "Divert them. At least *one* of them. Improve the odds."

"But how?"

"Get closer!" Kasha instructed Boon.

"Do it," Durgen agreed.

"Yah!" Boon got the zenzens moving again.

Kasha clambered onto the driver's seat with Boon. She hunkered down on her haunches, preparing. With a burst of energy, she pushed off with her powerful back legs and leaped onto the back of one of the galloping zenzens. It let out a startled whinny and bucked, but she hung on. She crawled forward so she could sit up on its back in a proper riding position, clinging to the zenzen's heaving flanks with her legs.

"Go left!" she cried.

Boon yanked the reins and the zenzen responded. Kasha twisted around to face the cart. "Throw me a spear!"

Durgen stood and flung her a weapon. Kasha caught it neatly and faced forward again. She flipped the spear around and used the handle to prod a nearby gar.

"Go!" she shouted at it. "Straight!" She began herding

the gars closer to the tang. Despite their terror of the tangs, the thundering hooves and the snarling klee baring her teeth and claws made them obey.

"Hey!" Kasha shouted at the tangs. "Over here! Dinner!"

The tangs turned to look, just as Kasha had hoped.

"Gars!" she shouted. "Run away as fast as you can!" She swiped the air with the spear, sending half the group she'd corralled in one direction, and the other half the opposite way.

One of the tangs took off after a group of gars. It pounced on a stumbling gar, knocking it to the ground. It opened its drooling mouth wide, its second set of fangs glistening, and went to work on the gar.

The other tang paused for a moment, and its indecision gave Flor the opening he needed. He grabbed a spear and sent it deep into the tang's flesh.

Kasha hurtled her flying disc at the tang. It sliced neatly into the back of its neck.

The tang jerked up and let out a howl. As it flung its head back to screech, Kasha flung another disc at it, this time slicing right into its throat.

Boon slowed the zenzens to a stop. Kasha brought her breathing back to normal as she dismounted.

"Any more?" Durgen called to Flor.

Flor shook his head, too winded to speak.

"Home?" Boon asked.

"I think we're safe from here." Durgen ordered the remaining gars to pick up the sacks and load the carts. They avoided looking at the dead as they went about their work.

"Thanks," Flor called to Kasha.

"You would do the same for me," she replied.

Kasha sat on the edge of the cart as it rumbled out of the field, heading back to Leeandra. Exhausted gars trundled alongside the cart, blood- and mud-spattered.

"You did well," Durgen said to Kasha. He wasn't one to give compliments, so Kasha knew she had particularly impressed him. "You saved Flor and much of the harvest."

She shrugged. "If we don't forage well, everyone suffers. Even the gars."

"Your dedication is something to be proud of," Durgen said. "You set a good example. Particularly for one so young. You are your father's daughter."

Kasha took in a deep breath and let it out again. More than anything, that last compliment was the one that pleased her.

Still, she kept her eyes firmly focused forward as they lumbered along the path to the main road through the dense jungle. She didn't want to see the casualties. She knew it was the way of things—tangs attacked and klees had to use all weapons at hand to protect themselves and the harvest, even if that meant losing gars. *Most of them got away*, she reminded herself. The losses would have been greater if she hadn't been so quick to act.

Much worse for everyone.

Two

"You should have seen her!" Boon said to Seegen, Kasha's father. "I think she actually jumped over my head to land on the back of that zenzen."

Kasha smiled and shook her head. "I did what I had to do."

"I worry that you take such risks," Seegen said.

"Maybe so," Kasha teased, "but everything I know about fighting tangs I learned from you!"

Boon feigned shock. "And I thought *I* had been your mentor!"

After the forage Kasha and Boon had cleaned up and then met again to go to Seegen's home near the center of Leeandra, the city built high in the trees of the jungle. Boon and Kasha had been friends since childhood, and Kasha and her father both thought of Boon as a member of their family. Admittedly, sometimes Boon seemed like a pesky younger brother Kasha wished she never had, but those times were few and far between.

"I am proud of you." Seegen leaned forward and brushed Kasha's furred cheek with his. Kasha felt as if she were glowing inside. "Being a forager is a vital service. But a father cannot help but worry about a daughter."

"It's the tangs who need to worry about Kasha!" Boon said. "That was a brilliant idea, sending those two groups of gars in opposite directions. The tangs took the bait."

Seegen looked at Kasha. "The gars were killed?"

Kasha shrugged. "Some were. Some usually are."

"You chose to sacrifice the gars as a fighting strategy?" Seegen asked.

Kasha didn't understand her father's reaction. He knew what was required when foraging. Survival was never a sure thing for any of the participants—gar or klee. Kasha felt her fur bristle. "Gars are killed during forages. So are klees. Tangs do not discriminate. We're all meat to them."

Boon must have been surprised by Seegen's question as well.

"Kasha's quick thinking saved us—," Boon began.

"And gars," Kasha pointed out.

"And protected most of the harvest," Boon finished.

"Yes, yes. That is all to the good," Seegen said. "I suppose I am just always troubled by the bloodshed."

"Tell it to the tangs," Kasha said flatly. She tapped the table with her paw.

"I am sure you did what you thought was right," Seegen said. "I know how seriously you take your work."

Kasha nodded, but that flush of pleasure she'd felt only a moment before had evaporated.

"Hello?" A large, elderly klee entered the tree house. His long fur had turned gray with age, and he moved carefully.

"Yorn! Come in! You are just in time for dinner!" Seegen greeted his old friend.

"Funny, he seems to always arrive around this time," Boon whispered to Kasha.

"Just like you," Kasha teased. "Somehow you always appear in time for a meal!"

"Boon and Kasha were just telling me about today's forage," Seegen said.

"Ahhh," Yorn said, taking a seat at the table. "Many losses?"

"Kasha kept down the casualties," Boon said before Seegen or Kasha could respond. "Durgen was very impressed."

"You do Leeandra a great service," Yorn told Kasha. "But I would expect nothing less from Seegen's daughter. Perhaps she, too, will have a seat on the council some day."

Kasha looked at her father with excitement. "You're going to be named to the Council of Klee?"

Seegen smiled. "Nothing is certain, but there has been some talk."

"Be assured, Seegen," Yorn said. "It will happen. Who is more deserving? Why, you practically built Leeandra all on your own. From hollowing out the enormous trees in order to build the elevators to designing the rail system that runs alongside the sky bridges."

Seegen shook his head with a grin. "You give me too much credit."

"He's right," Kasha said. "This is an honor that should have come to you ages ago."

"I have been honored simply by the talk," Seegen said. "From the beginning I believed in Leeandra. That is why I did all I could to help it grow and thrive. I still do. We have a great future ahead of us."

"I believe in dinner," Boon declared. "Dinner would be a great future." His brown snout wrinkled as he sniffed. His whiskers twitched. "And from the smell of things, that future is now."

"I'll get the food," Kasha said. "Or Boon may go tang on us!"

Boon growled and bared his teeth. He lunged for Kasha, but she neatly sidestepped him. Boon sprawled on the floor, laughing.

Kasha shook her head. Sometimes she wondered whether Boon was ever serious about anything! Still, he was a good friend, and she knew he would always have her back. And she knew he felt the same way about her.

"Come on, scary beast." Kasha held out her paw to help Boon up.

"Yes," Yorn said with a smile. "Let us old folks talk a bit. You two have too much energy for me. You're tiring me out just watching you!"

Boon and Kasha padded out to the kitchen as Yorn was saying, "This council seat means that you could work to make some of those changes you have been talking about. . . ."

"Do you really think he will get a seat on the council soon?" Kasha asked once they were in the kitchen.

Boon pulled plates from their shelves. "I think it's a sure thing. Then you'll be the daughter of a council leader."

"A lot of good that will do me," Kasha joked, putting roasted meat onto a large serving platter. "He will probably make things harder on me just to prove he's not showing favoritism."

"You're probably right about that," Boon said. "But you wouldn't have it any other way."

Kasha smiled. "True." Her father's integrity was one of the many qualities she admired. And she knew her own desire to earn her way, rather than having anything handed to her, was a quality of hers that made her father proud.

"Now that smells good!" Yorn declared as Kasha and Boon re-entered the room.

Kasha put the platter in the center of the table while Boon passed out the plates. Soon the heaping platter of meat had dwindled to just one slice.

Kasha's amber eyes met Boon's dark brown ones. Both whipped out their paws to swipe it, but Kasha was quicker. The tasty morsel was already in her mouth as Boon's paw hit the platter.

"Mm-mm," Kasha said. She licked her paws and grinned.

Boon laughed. "Those reflexes—it's why I knew you would be great at wippen."

Kasha's eyes flicked to her father. He had objected when she joined the wippen team. It was still a sore point between them. Yorn looked uncomfortable. It was obvious he knew what her father's position was on the game.

"This year's tournament is going great!" Boon continued, obviously unaware of the discomfort at the table. "Coach Jorsa is really pleased with Kasha's performance."

"I wish you would reconsider, Kasha," Seegen said.

Boon looked shocked. "But she's so good! We're sure to win with Kasha on our team! Why would you want her to quit?"

"My father thinks wippen is wrong," Kasha said.

"How can a game be wrong?" Boon asked.

Seegen cleared his throat. "It is unfair to use the gars as expendable game equipment."

"Klees can get injured as well," Kasha argued.

"It is a traditional game," Yorn pointed out. "My father was a coach back in the old times."

"Just because something is as it always has been does not make it right," Seegen said.

"The gar players are well fed and well cared for," Kasha insisted. Why would her father not see that this wasn't a problem?

"Boon agrees with me on this," Kasha said. "Right, Boon?"

Boon stood to clear the dishes. "I . . . well . . . I . . ."

"And so does everyone else," Kasha continued. "It is the way of things."

"I thought I taught you better than that," Seegen said.

Kasha stared at her father, stung. "Wh-What do you mean?"

"I raised you to think for yourself," Seegen admonished her. "Not just take on the attitudes of those around you."

"Of course I think for myself!" Kasha protested. How could her own father insult her this way? "If I did not, I would simply agree with *you*!"

Now Seegen smiled. "I suppose you are right. A less strong-minded person would parrot my opinion back to me. But I do wish you would think more about your positions. Question your own assumptions—and those held by others."

Kasha swallowed. "I promise to keep a more open mind on the subject of gars and wippen," she said finally. She didn't really think she'd change her opinion, but she would at least consider her father's point of view. "But will you keep an open mind too?"

Seegen placed his paw over Kasha's. "Agreed. That is only fair."

"So you will come to the game and cheer our team?" she asked.

"You must!" Boon exclaimed. "With Kasha on our side we have a shot at the championship this year!"

Seegen looked from Boon to Kasha. "I can see this means a lot to you."

Kasha nodded. "It does."

"Then I will be there, daughter. If it is important to you, it is important to me."

"Excellent!" Boon said. "Yorn, you should come too. The more cheering us on from the stands the better."

"I would not miss it!" Yorn said. "Not with both of you playing."

Kasha felt better. She was sure when her father saw her play, he'd change his mind. She would prove to him that wippen was a grand sport—a game of honor and skill. She'd make him as proud of her performance on the wippen field as he was of her work as a forager.

THREE

Kasha lapped up water greedily. Her fur was matted with sweat. She'd played hard, and they were taking their first and only break in the wippen game.

"Looking good out there!" Boon said.

Kasha nodded. She felt it too. The team was in complete synch, moving as if they were one mind, one body. And she was really on her game today.

She paced back and forth in the Blue Team break area. She needed to keep her muscles warm and her focus sharp. Wippen took physical strength, skill, quick reflexes, and good strategy.

She gazed around the stadium. The huge arena was packed. They were nearing the end of the tournament, and each game had higher stakes than the last one. These next three games between Kasha's Blue Team and the opposing Red Team would determine who won the championship.

Seats were filled all the way to the bamboo walls that surrounded the grassy field. To one side was the corral holding the zenzens the klees rode; on the other side was the area where the gars waited to enter the game.

Each team began with twenty gars—ten on the field and ten as backup. Gars were used to steal or pass the ball, and as goalies. Only klees could actually make goals, and they could steal from one another, so gars were also used to block and clear paths for the klees atop the zenzens. As they tired or were injured, new gars would be sent in. In particularly heated games, teams could find themselves without gars at all by the end, forcing the klee players to battle it all out on zenzens. Injuries were common—more among gars, but plenty of klees got hurt too.

The Blue Team coach, Jorsa, strode into the break area. "The Red Team's forward klees are stronger riders than passers," she said. "Force them to pass to their teammates."

"The gars are doing their passing for them," Kasha said.

"Exactly," Jorsa said. "We take out the gars, we put them in a weaker position."

"Got it!" Kasha said.

"You and Boon are our strongest riders," Jorsa continued. "You keep the forwards from being able to pass the ball."

Kasha glanced up into the stands. She hadn't risked checking to see if her father was here before—she'd been too nervous. She wasn't sure if she wanted to find him out there or not. She would have been disappointed to discover he hadn't come, but if he was here, she'd feel even more pressure to play well.

There he was, sitting with Yorn. This was the very first time he had ever come to a game. He really *was* keeping an open mind. She tingled under her fur with pride.

Now he'd see what an exciting game this was, and that there was nothing wrong with it. Good. She was glad she had looked. Energy surged through her. She was ready for the final half.

"Everyone, remount your zenzens!" Jorsa called.

Kasha retrieved her "scoop"—the long-handled stick with a net attached at one end. She'd use this to catch, carry, and throw the ball. She could also use the handle to knock the ball out of an opposing player's scoop or a gar's hands.

Kasha climbed back up onto her zenzen. *In a way*, she mused, *foraging is good training for wippen—and vice versa*. Both activities required keen awareness, teamwork, quick reflexes, and great riding ability. Maybe her father would see that as well.

The horn blew, indicating the break was over. Kasha was ready.

"Go in for the face-off," Jorsa told Kasha.

"Me?" Kasha hadn't expected that, but she was honored. That meant the coach really thought she was good.

Kasha rode the zenzen to the center of the field and faced her opponent from the Red Team.

The other player was a light-furred female. Her green eyes narrowed and her ears flattened as she faced Kasha. The player gripped her scoop. Kasha clutched hers and pressed her legs into the zenzen's flanks. She leaned forward, lifting her seat slightly out of the saddle so she was ready to move in any direction.

Kasha's teammates rode to their positions around the field. The Red Team players did the same. Gars scattered across the field. They knew if they played well, they'd be rewarded with extra food and treats; if they did poorly, they'd be off the team and lose the privileges that came with being players. All players—gar and klee alike—faced the risks of the fast-moving, highly competitive game.

Zenzens snorted and stamped hooves, impatient to begin. Kasha was impatient too.

Tweeeeeeeeeeeeeeeeeeeeet!

The whistle blew; the game master tossed the ball into the air between Kasha and her Red Team opponent. The final round was on!

Kasha raced at the ball with her scoop raised. She stood in the stirrups and stretched up—got it! The ball landed in her net.

The Red Team player charged her, and Kasha hurled the ball to the gar open on the left side of the field. Then she raced her zenzen into position near the goal.

The gar swooped up the ball and was instantly pounced on by several Red Team gars. Two zenzens thundered toward the pile of gars, and they scattered, not wanting to be trampled.

Kasha's gar still clutched the ball. He rolled quickly out of the path of the oncoming hooves and flung the ball away from him. The ball rolled along the ground, and Boon and a Red Team player thundered toward it. Gars from both teams raced alongside them, trying to block. A Red Team gar grabbed the ball and ran to drop it into the net of his teammate's scoop.

Boon used the handle of his scoop and tried to knock the ball out of the gar's hand. His scoop hit the gar, who went down, dropping the ball.

Boon swooped it up and threw it high and true. "Kasha!" he cried.

Kasha stood in her stirrups and caught it neatly in her net.

None of her teammates were in good positions for her to pass. She whistled and one of her team gars dashed over to her. She threw him the ball so he could run with it. He darted in and out of zenzens and gars. He wasn't allowed to score, but he could maneuver the ball into a better spot. Red Team players went after him, and he, too, went down, losing the ball.

"Boon!" Kasha pointed toward the ball with her scoop.

"On it!" Boon shouted. He swooped in, picked it up, and galloped toward the goal.

Score!

There was no time to celebrate. Another ball was sent into play and a Red Team gar grabbed it.

The two teams battled it out. Each gained control of the ball, then lost it; each won a point, pulling into the lead only to have the other team match it. Soon it was the final quarter, and the teams were tied.

A ball was sent into play.

Kasha charged for it. She whistled for gars to protect her as she thundered toward the goal.

"Cover me!" she ordered. She held her scoop high,

keeping the ball aloft. Gars flanked her as she rode her zenzen hard to the far side of the field. Red Team gars and klees knocked them out of the way, desperate to reach her. This was the deciding moment.

Kasha's eyes flicked to the stands. She wanted her father to see her make the tie-breaking goal.

Her father—he was frowning.

Was he worried she wouldn't make the goal? Or was this disapproval? Injured gars were being carried off the field. *But that's normal*, she told herself. *And injured klees were taken out by their coaches at the break.*

Kasha was suddenly thrown off balance, and the ball tipped out of her net.

What just happened?

Then she realized—a Red Team gar had jumped up and yanked her stirrups. Kasha watched in dismay as a Red Team klee quickly scooped up the ball and galloped across the field.

"Yah!" Kasha shouted, and kicked her zenzen hard. She raced after the ball.

The Red Team klee passed the ball to a gar positioned near the goal.

Time to charge!

Kasha urged the zenzen forward. "Got it!" she shouted to her teammates. "Get ready!" She knew just what to do: slam the gar so it couldn't get close to the goal.

The zenzen reacted to every move she made, the way she leaned, the flick of the reins. The gar thought he had the field—most of Kasha's Blue Team was still at the other end, near their own goal. It was up to her.

"Yah!" she cried again.

The gar heard her this time and glanced back at her.

The gar froze, his face filled with terror as Kasha thundered toward him, ready to move in to steal the ball. It was a perfect setup. Knock him down and grab it. She'd easily throw it to her teammates who dotted the field ready to receive.

Almost there . . . almost there . . . and . . .

She yanked hard on the reins and pulled the zenzen to a stop. She stopped so suddenly, she nearly flew over the front of the saddle.

The gar blinked, then quickly hurled the ball to the Red Team klee positioned just in front of the goal.

Score for the Red Team!

The final and winning point.

It all happened so quickly. Dazed, Kasha slumped in the saddle as the Red Team and their fans cheered.

She could have won the game for her team. Instead she lost it.

She could kick herself. What was *wrong* with her? First she lost the ball by being distracted. Then—and this was the craziest thing of all—she actually *stopped* herself from using a classic wippen strategy: knock down the gar and steal the ball. She was all set up for it. But she stopped!

If she hadn't hesitated, her Blue Team would be enjoying the winners' ride around the stadium. Instead, they were slinking out to return the zenzens to the corral.

"You okay?" Boon asked.

Kasha didn't respond. She climbed down from the zenzen and began its grooming.

Boon dismounted and patted his zenzen's sweaty and heaving flanks. "So, what happened out there?"

"I messed up," Kasha snapped.

"But you never mess up," Boon pressed. "You just stopped out there! Inches from the gar!"

"I lost focus, okay? It won't happen again."

"It better not," Jorsa said as she walked into the stable. "I took a chance on you, Kasha, putting you in these final games. You're a new player. But you have always been so strong, so intent on winning—"

"It was one game!" Kasha insisted. "One error."

"An important game. At the critical moment."

"I know! I let you all down. I won't let it happen again."

"You are right you won't. I will not let you have the chance," Jorsa said.

"What do you mean?" Kasha asked.

"I'll have to think about whether or not to put you in the next game." Jorsa stalked out of the stall.

Kasha stared after her. She felt terrible. She'd let the team down. And her father had watched the whole thing.

FOUR

One week later Kasha held very still in the Blue Team's area, waiting for Jorsa's decision. She had been tense all week, anticipating this moment. She didn't have the right to insist on being put in the game; she knew she'd let the team down last week. But she hoped she'd be allowed to prove herself.

"Give her another chance, Jorsa," Boon said. "Kasha will play better today, I know it."

Jorsa looked from Boon to Kasha. "Do *you* know it?" she asked Kasha.

Kasha gave a sharp nod. "Yes. I think I know why I faltered. I—I made sure it won't happen again."

Kasha was convinced it was concern about her father's reaction to the game that had distracted her. So she asked him not to attend any more games and—not surprisingly—he agreed. He still wasn't a fan of wippen. He just wouldn't budge on it. At least he wasn't going to try to get her to quit—he acknowledged he was in the minority opinion on the popular game. And, as Kasha reminded him, he raised her to make her own choices.

Jorsa studied Kasha for a moment, then said, "All right. I will start you, but I might not keep you in."

"Thank you," Kasha said. "I won't let you down."

Boon and Kasha headed for the corral to get their zenzens.

"This is great!" Boon declared. "She's putting you in!" Boon was full of energy, practically bouncing as they walked. "Remember to keep the scoop high," he said. "And when in doubt, pass—even to a gar. Also—"

"I know," Kasha snapped. "I have played before. I only messed up that one time."

"Sorry," Boon said. "It's just that this game is really important and—"

"I know that too!" Kasha picked up her scoop and then hoisted herself up onto her zenzen's back. She leaned forward in the saddle and urged her zenzen onto the field. All of Boon's chatter was only making her nervous. She knew he meant well, but she was having a hard time keeping herself from knocking him with her scoop.

The rest of the Blue Team trotted onto the field. A few glanced at her then looked away. Kasha tightened her grip on her scoop. She knew she had to earn back their respect. She would.

"Boon!" Jorsa called. "Face-off."

Boon grinned and trotted toward center field. The game master tossed the ball and Boon and the Red Team player raced toward it. Both players stood in their stirrups holding up the scoops. The zenzens thundered toward each other.

Kasha held her breath—she had to be ready to respond. *Focus*, she told herself. *Focus and*—

The Red Team got the ball!

Boon used the handle of his scoop to try to knock the ball out of the Red Team player's net, but the player flung the ball to one of his own team's gars. A Blue Team gar intercepted it and threw it to a Blue Team klee.

Kasha flicked the reins and raced her zenzen to a forward position. "Open!" she cried.

The player looked around the field and tossed the ball to a gar. The gar took off running. A Blue Team player rode up next to the gar, who dropped it into the net of the scoop.

Three Red Team gars and a Red Team klee raced after Kasha's teammate. He was surrounded.

"Over here!" Kasha shouted.

Her boxed-in teammate glanced her way, then threw the ball to Boon.

That makes no sense, Kasha thought. *He just sent the ball backward.* "Boon!" she called.

Boon turned to look at her. He raised his scoop for the throw, but a Red Team player knocked the ball out of Boon's net. A pile of gars threw themselves onto the ball. Zenzens stomped around them until a Red Team gar managed to extricate himself from the pile. As the gar stumbled away, Boon knocked the ball out of his hands. Boon couldn't reach the ball to stake it, but he managed to hit it with his scoop hard enough to roll it to another Blue Team player. She scooped it up and yanked on her zenzen's reins, making it turn sharply.

"I can take it!" Kasha cried. She was just yards from the goal.

The Blue Player ignored her and galloped toward the goal. Gars scattered to avoid being trampled.

Kasha blinked. She couldn't believe it. No one would pass to her! *If they're not going to use me, there's no point in my being in the game.* She didn't know if she was hurt or furious.

She kicked her zenzen's flanks and raced into center field. Since no one would send her the ball, she'd have to go and get it.

She heard a snort and a whinny behind her. A gar had spooked the zenzen heading toward the goal, throwing the Blue Team klee rider. The ball fell from the scoop and Kasha saw her chance.

She galloped toward the ball. A Red Team gar grabbed it, and Kasha used her scoop to knock it out of his hands. He clung to the ball and she swung again. She heard him cry out and felt the dull *thunk* of her scoop hitting flesh, but she kept her eyes on the ball. The gar dropped it and Kasha quickly scooped it up.

"Yah! Yah! Yah!" she shouted, kicking her zenzen hard. Her shouts spurred on her zenzen, but it also startled the gars—they flung themselves out of her way.

Kasha forced the zenzen to run straight at the goal—and the gar goalie. At the last moment, the gar threw himself out of her path. Kasha yanked on the reins sharply, pulling the zenzen to a sudden stop, its hooves sending clumps of dirt flying. Kasha hurled in the ball.

Score!

She trotted back to the center field. *Maybe now they'll pass to me*, she thought.

"Ball in play!" the game master shouted.

The Red Team took control of the ball. Kasha saw where the pass would happen. She raced her zenzen in for a block. The ball went high, and Kasha stood in the stirrups to reach it. She miscalculated, and the ball hit her in the head with a loud *thwack*.

Her body slid sideways from the force of the blow, but she managed to stay in the saddle. She shook her head to clear it and was pleased to see that the ball was being carried by a Blue Team gar.

The gar tossed the ball to Boon, who neatly swooped it up and threw it into the goal. Another score.

"Ball in play!"

Kasha tossed the scoop from paw to paw. Her muscles felt warm from exertion, fluid, strong. Her senses were alert, acute. *Nothing but the game*. Total focus.

"Pass!" she cried, as she watched gars chasing the ball down the field. A Red Team gar threw the ball, but Boon intercepted it. He threw it to Kasha. The two friends galloped down the field tossing the ball back and forth as gars raced after them. Red Team players rode hard between them, but Boon and Kasha were able to keep control of the ball.

A Red Team player rode up beside Kasha. When she aimed her scoop to throw the ball back to Boon, the Red Team player knocked it out of her net. Kasha tried to catch it again, and she and her opponent fought it out. Gars from both teams also tried to steal the ball. Kasha and the Red Team player knocked into the gars as they struggled for possession of the ball, but finally a Blue Team gar wrestled it away. He ran with it and threw it to Boon. . . .

And score!

The horn blew, and it was time for the break. Panting nearly as hard as her zenzen, Kasha rode off the field.

Jorsa stood smiling at the water station. "Well, you certainly made up for last week."

"Thanks," Kasha said. "Boon is playing well today too."

Boon rode up beside her. "I liked that special block you did. That was really using your *head*." He slid sideways, mimicking being hit in the head with a wippen ball.

"Ha-ha." Kasha grinned at him. "You should try it. Knock some sense into you."

As she gave her zenzen water, she watched injured gars being pulled off the field. "The Red Team lost a lot of gars."

"Good," Jorsa said. "It weakens their team. They won't have as many as we do."

"They may try to take down ours. Even up the odds," Boon said.

"Do we defend them?" Kasha asked, trying to figure out a good second-half strategy.

"No," Jarsa said. "Gars play defense for *us*, not the other way around. We use them that way as long as we have them."

"The Red Team is going to play even harder to try to catch up," Boon said. "We will need to be ready."

Jarsa pulled two players out who'd been hurt in the

game and sent in two fresh replacements. "What about me?" Kasha asked.

"You up for it?"

"Yes."

"Then you're back in."

Energy surged through Kasha, thrilled she'd proven herself. She was ready. She paced the break area on all fours, eager to get back into the game.

"Kasha, face-off!"

Kasha mounted her zenzen. This round would determine everything. If the Blue Team lost the game, the championship would be over today. The Red Team would have won two out of three. Both sides were going to play hard. Kasha had no doubt the second half would be a lot rougher and result in any number of injuries—klee and gar alike.

Well, Kasha thought as she trotted the zenzen onto the field. *We'll just play smarter.*

Kasha faced her Red Team opponent. It was the same green-eyed klee she had faced before. Her ears flattened when she saw she was going up against Kasha. She sat high in the saddle, not even holding the reins, keeping both paws on her scoop.

Kasha smiled. She liked how fiercely her opponent tried to stare her down. That meant she viewed Kasha as a formidable player—a powerhouse. Exactly as Kasha wanted to see herself.

Kasha heard the Red Team player let out a low, throaty growl. "Don't be so sure of yourself," she snarled at Kasha.

Kasha just continued to smile. She was determined

to prove Jorsa hadn't made a mistake putting her in, despite the loss last week. The other team's aggressive stance didn't scare her, it only fueled her confidence.

"In play!" the game master shouted, tossing the ball. Kasha swooped it up in her net. The Red Team player's scoop came down hard on Kasha's, but Kasha didn't lose control of the ball. She angled her scoop, deftly keeping the ball from falling out of the net, and yanked her zenzen's reins. It made a hard right turn and took off.

Kasha was instantly surrounded by Red Team gars on foot and klees on zenzens. It was as if they knew she'd win the face-off. She scanned the field. She had to pass—and fast!

Boon had Red Team players shadowing him; she'd have to look elsewhere. The Red Team had clearly indentified her and Boon as the major threats here.

I'll have to change strategy, she thought, pulling her scoop close in to her body to protect the ball. This was risky: Klees determined to knock the ball out of her net could easily whack her with their scoops, and it wouldn't be called a foul.

Kasha glanced over her shoulder, then twisted in the saddle. She hurled the ball toward a Blue Team gar behind her.

Startled by the surprising pass, the Blue Team gar fumbled and dropped the ball. Luckily, none of the Red Team was nearby—they had all raced into position near the goal. The gar quickly recovered and ran the ball into a good position to pass to another klee player.

Before the ball made it to the goal, a Blue Team gar was pulled out due to an injury after a Red Team zenzen stomped on the gar's foot as the klee player frantically tried changing direction. The ball was sent back into play, and the Blue Team scored.

Keep them confused, Kasha decided. *Never let the Red Team predict where the ball will be.*

Ball after ball went into play, and each time the Blue Team scored, the Red Team fought back even more aggressively.

The Red Team was down in gars, so the klee players were doing most of the blocking themselves. This was an added danger as the huge zenzens barreled down on one another. This gave Kasha an idea.

It was down to the winning point. Kasha's muscles ached, and she knew she'd be bruised tomorrow. A nasty scratch across the top of her paw had left blood on her fur. She wasn't even sure how it had happened.

Kasha gained control of the ball. *Make it count,* she told herself.

Over and over she passed the ball to the gars in all directions, forward, backward, right and left. Her teammates followed her lead, and they, too, passed the ball right back to the gars. The Red Team couldn't play offense *or* defense; they were having too much trouble figuring out where to look next.

Zenzens reared up, snorting and whinnying as Red Team klees crisscrossed the field. The Red Team hadn't just lost control of the ball, they were losing control of their zenzens as they forced them to continually shift, turn, stop, and charge in sudden, surprising bursts.

Kasha raced her zenzen on the outskirts of the field to the goal. The Red Team still saw her as the primary opponent and flanked her. She got the ball and threw it to a gar, who threw it to another gar. And another. The ball was heading back toward the Red Team's goal.

Kasha kicked her zenzen hard and raced back down the field. She knocked the ball out of a Red Team gar's hands. She abruptly turned the zenzen and headed back the way she'd come. "Stay with me!" she shouted to two gars. They ran alongside her as she thundered toward the goal.

She shut out the sounds around her; the crowd's cheers and boos, the zenzen's snorting, the shouts of players, the thudding of powerful hooves. She shut out everything but the path opening up before her to the goal. She urged her zenzen to gallop faster, straighter. She was breathing hard, in time with her zenzen's hooves hitting the dirt.

She was aware of other zenzens stomping toward her, of bodies all around her, but she kept her eyes straight ahead, her only focus on the goal and protecting the ball. No more passing now—she was bringing this one home.

She heard a loud cry and a shout, and some kind of commotion in the stands just as she hurled in the ball.

Score!

She did it! Kasha took in a deep breath and slumped in the saddle, the tension easing out of her. That was it. That was the winning goal. They were still in the championship.

She slowly turned her zenzen around, allowing it to settle into a walk.

She joined the rest of the Blue Team's victory circle

around the stadium. Although her teammates were holding their scoops high in victory, and the crowd was applauding, what caught her eye was the gar holding pen. There was something going on.

Gradually she understood what she was seeing. A gar was being dragged off the field, but he wasn't injured, he was dead.

Trampled by a zenzen, Kasha figured. That was the cause of most of the more serious gar injuries. The klees were all riding in close quarters at the last point and zenzens had been getting spooked all around her.

Although uncommon, the death wasn't the surprise. What struck Kasha was the reaction of a female gar in the holding pen.

A female in filthy rags was wailing as if she herself were in tormented pain. She flung herself onto the body of the dead gar. Her deep anguish was palpable; Kasha felt tears sting her eyes even though she didn't really understand what she was watching. What was clear was the death of this gar had unhinged the female.

A klee guard grabbed the female to remove her so that the field could be cleared. The female kicked out at the guard, and her obvious grief transformed into rage. The guard hit her with a stick, and several gars ran to her, pulling her away from the dead gar. Her shrieks chilled Kasha, and she found herself needing to look away as the female wept and screamed, her pale, thin, and dirty arms reaching desperately for the dead gar.

How strange, Kasha thought, disturbed by the scene. *It's as if the gars have feelings just like the klees.*

FIVE

You were amazing!" Boon gushed as he and Kasha left the wippen stadium after the game. They stepped into the elevator headed for the monorail that ringed the city of Leeandra. They'd take it to city center, and then from there, they would walk the rest of the way to Seegen's home for their weekly dinner.

"I guess. . . ." Kasha watched the small wooden houses dotting the gigantic trees as the elevator brought them up to higher levels. It stopped, and they stepped onto the crowded platform.

"What's wrong?" Boon asked. "You've been awfully quiet ever since the game ended. Are you injured?"

"What?" Kasha turned to look at Boon. The thick canopy of foliage above them cast shadows across his face despite the warm glow emitted by the streetlights. She realized she hadn't heard a word he had said.

Boon frowned. "Are you all right? You should be purring with pride. Thanks to you we're still in the running for the championship! You tied us with the Red Team."

"I—I am just tired."

They stepped into the monorail.

"Of course, you're tired," Boon said. "You played a powerful game. Here, take this seat."

Kasha sat, her haunches aching from the earlier exertion. She'd worked her muscles hard, clinging to the zenzen, reaching, throwing, twisting. But it wasn't fatigue that had her so quiet or distracted.

Kasha stared at the leafy branches brushing the monorail window. She couldn't get the image of the distraught gar female out of her mind. The screaming. The weeping.

"You'll feel better after one of your father's feasts," Boon said.

"That gar who was killed . . . ," Kasha began. She stopped herself. She wasn't sure what she wanted to ask. She had never thought of gars as having families before, but that's what she felt she'd seen: a gar who had lost her mate, and who felt it as deeply as her own father had at the loss of her mother.

Could that be true?

"It's been a long time since a gar was killed during a game," Boon commented. "Those Red Team players really were getting out of control at the end there."

"Here we are," Kasha said. She got up and sprinted out of the monorail. They would take sky bridges from here.

"For someone so exhausted, you sure are keeping a quick pace," Boon complained. "Slow down. I played hard too."

"Sorry."

"Hey, is that your father?"

Kasha looked at the nearby elevator. Boon was right. Seegen was stepping out of it and onto the sky bridge. Boon and Kasha hurried over to greet him.

"Hello, Father," Kasha said. "What are you doing in this part of the city?"

Seegen blinked a few times, as if he were having trouble placing them. Then he smiled. "Kasha, Boon. I could ask you the same thing."

"We just took the monorail from the wippen stadium," Boon said. "Kasha really made up for last week's game today. You should have seen her play. The way she—"

"That game!" Seegen spat. "It should be outlawed."

Boon quickly looked to Kasha, obviously surprised by the vehemence of Seegen's reaction. He also seemed worried that he'd said the wrong thing.

Were they going to have this argument again? "I thought you were going to keep an open mind," Kasha said.

Seegen's dark eyes grew misty. "So many things to think about," he murmured. "To rethink."

"What are you talking about?" Kasha asked.

"This world . . ." Seegen's voice trailed off.

Kasha had never seen her father like this. So preoccupied. So confused. "Are you all right?"

"I—I do not know. Yes. Yes. I am fine. I am . . . more than fine. I am just . . ."

"Sir, do you think—," Boon began.

Kasha cut him off. "Father, Boon won't be able to join us for dinner tonight."

"Dinner?" Seegen repeated.

"No?" Boon looked at Kasha quizzically.

Kasha shot Boon a warning glare. She needed to be alone with her father. He was acting so strangely—she didn't want anyone, not even Boon, to see him like this.

Boon got the silent message. "Right. I won't be able to join you. Things to do."

"Yes . . . things to do. So many things to do. To make right," Seegen said. "To learn."

Kasha watched dumbfounded as her father's expression changed from bewilderment to exhilaration.

"Oh, Daughter! There is so much for us to talk about." He clapped his large paws onto her shoulders. She could feel him quivering with excitement.

"Yes, we will go home and talk," Kasha said.

She turned to Boon. She hated the worried look on his face. She didn't want anyone to feel sorry for her or her father.

"See you at the forage tomorrow," she said.

"Till tomorrow." Boon turned and headed back toward the monorail.

Seegen stood at the rail of the sky bridge looking out over the thick treetops of the jungle. "It is beautiful. I should notice it more often. Why do we take it all for granted?"

"I—I don't know," Kasha replied. "Let's go." If Seegen was ill, she didn't want him in the city center. He should be at home, where she and Yorn could take care of him.

"Home." Seegen seemed to savor the word. "What a lovely sound. What a lovely concept."

Kasha slipped her arm through her father's and hurried him along as best she could. Every now and then he'd stop to sniff the air or to gaze lovingly at some tree or view.

Kasha's heart grew heavy. *Is he dying? Is that why he's behaving this way?*

"You sit," Kasha said as they entered Seegen's home. "I will prepare dinner."

Kasha went into the kitchen and stood staring blankly at the food containers. Something was happening to her father, and she had no idea what.

She shook herself out of her fear. She piled platters with food and drink and brought it all out to her father. He stood gazing out the large windows.

She moved slowly—she could feel her muscles tightening after the intense playing she'd done earlier.

"Are you all right?" he asked, turning around.

"Me?" Kasha said. "I'm worried about *you*."

"You're favoring your left side."

"It was a rough game," Kasha said, placing the platter on the table.

"Game!" Seegen snarled. "It is no game. It's a form of abuse!"

Stunned, Kasha took a step back.

"Our whole society is based on the exploitation of the gars," Seegen railed. "We must put a stop to it."

"What are you talking about?"

"We treat them as if they were nothing more than animals, existing solely for our use."

"But—" Kasha stopped herself. Gars were there for the klees to use. They served a purpose in klee society and always had. Why would her father be so adamant about this? He was even more vehement about his disapproval now than he had been last week. Had something happened?

"Listen to me, Kasha," Seegen said. He took her paw and brought her to the sofa.

"What is that?" Kasha asked. She noticed he was wearing a cord around his neck with a large ring dangling from it. The ring had some kind of stone in the center, and what looked like etchings all around the stone. She'd never seen it before.

Seegen looked down at the ring. He took a moment before answering. "It is a gift. And a responsibility."

"The ring is a responsibility?" Nothing her father was saying was making any sense.

"I had an extraordinary experience today," Seegen said. He stood and paced. "I met someone very . . . unusual."

"Who?" Perhaps this meeting would explain her father's odd behavior. Could he have met with some of the Council of Klee?

"A gar. A gar named 'Press'."

"The gar had a name?" Kasha hadn't realized gars had names. Then she remembered that many families named their household gars. They often developed strong bonds with them. "Whose gar is it?"

"This gar is not owned by anyone."

"A rogue?"

"No! He is his own person. He is not like any gar I have ever known. Ever imagined." He shook his head. "Nothing is."

"Nothing is what?"

"As I thought."

"You're confusing me!" Kasha exploded. "You're not making any sense."

"I'm sorry. . . ." Seegen laughed. "I'm a bit confused myself. No, that is an understatement. I am completely confused—but exhilarated as well. To think of all those worlds . . ."

"Did this gar, this 'Press,' confuse you?" It was hard for Kasha to imagine that a creature of lesser intelligence could have set her father on this bizarre train of thought, but it seemed to be the only explanation.

"He opened my eyes!" Seegen declared.

"A gar?" She was still having trouble processing this. "How could a gar do that?"

"What he told me—"

"He spoke?" Now she simply stared at her father, completely flummoxed.

Seegen grew more animated. "He spoke, he laughed, he explained . . . so many things!" He looked straight at Kasha. "And he made me question everything!"

"A gar. Did all that?"

"And more!" Seegen dropped to all fours and paced. "I must find out all I can. I have to see him again."

Kasha stood. This had gone far enough. "Father, stop! If people hear you speaking this way, speaking against our society, of a special gar who changed your whole view of things . . . people will think you're mad! What if the council hears you? You'll never get a seat!"

Seegen stared at her as if she'd said something absurd. "A seat on the council? There are more important things than being named to council!"

"Like what? What has you so . . . so . . ." Kasha struggled to find the right word.

Seegen settled back onto his haunches. "I spoke too soon," Seegen said. "I realize that now. I do not know enough yet. Not nearly enough. When I know more, then, Daughter, I will tell you. Tell you everything."

He stared down at his new ring at the end of the cord.

"Fine," Kasha said. "I don't think I want to hear it anyway."

Seegen looked at her sadly. "I fear you won't be the only one. This will be a hard battle to fight."

"Now you're talking about a battle?" Kasha threw up her hands in exasperation.

"All at the right time," Seegen said. "The right time."

Six

Kasha rode the elevator inside the enormous hollow tree up to the forager operation center. Today she wasn't going out into the jungle to hunt or to the fields to harvest. No, today she was going to put in air hours. She was going to fly a gig.

She stepped off the elevator onto the circular balcony and followed it around to the tall arched doorway. She entered the enormous room that housed the gigs—the two-seater flying craft the foragers used.

"Hello, Kasha," Durgen greeted her. "I'll be flying with you today."

"Will you let me do the piloting this time?" Kasha asked. "Every time we go up together, you take the command chair."

"You're still new," Durgen argued.

"How will I learn if you don't let me take the lead?" Kasha demanded.

"You're right," Durgen admitted. "We can do this your way."

Kasha felt a thrill of excitement. Not only was she going to pilot, she had actually gotten Durgen to change his mind about something!

"What's the assignment?" Kasha asked as she and Durgen pushed a bright yellow gig to the launch platform.

"We're going to see if the fields are ripe in the far east," Durgen said. "No sense in a foraging team going all the way out there if the fruit isn't ready. We will pick up some things on the way back, too."

Durgen started to climb into the gig when Kasha stopped him.

"I am the pilot, remember?" she said with a grin.

"Sorry," Durgen said. "Habit."

Kasha slipped into the command chair. It felt good . . . right. She gripped the joystick that she'd use to control the gig. It fit perfectly in her paw.

So much seemed to be spinning into chaos and confusion. Her father's recent behavior, her own new and unsettled ideas about gars. What was right and what was wrong. She could push all those distracting and disturbing questions aside as she put all her attention on commanding this small craft.

Kasha toggled the power switches as Durgen took the copilot's seat. "Let me get in first," he complained.

"I know how you like to keep to a schedule," Kasha teased.

"Do not make me regret giving you this responsibility," Durgen said.

Kasha sighed. Why did she have to prove herself at every turn, to show that she wouldn't let people down?

Coach Jorsa, Durgen, even Boon, and her own father. Didn't they understand she pushed herself harder than anyone else could?

The overhead blades whined as they powered up. Kasha waited until Durgen was settled into the copilot chair and then grabbed the joystick between the two seats. She twisted it, and the gig raised off the platform and hovered a few inches above it.

"Are you comfortable?" Kasha asked Durgen in an overly solicitous tone. "May I please launch?"

"All right, all right," Durgen growled, but this time with humor. "Yes, take off."

Kasha turned another switch and the side rotors kicked in. The gig moved forward and Kasha gave it speed.

Kasha enjoyed feeling the surge of power as the gig launched into the air. The open cockpit allowed a strong breeze to carry the floral scent from the jungle to invigorate Kasha as she navigated the gig away from the launching area.

"So," Kasha said over the drone of the rotating blades. "East?"

"Take the same route we flew last week, and then I will guide you from there."

Kasha used the joystick to turn the gig, and pulled on the throttle to pick up speed. She would have loved to really put on the power, but knew that Durgen wouldn't approve. Even though they were friends, he was also her supervisor.

She was glad she had pulled gig rotation today. She didn't think she was up to facing tangs, or even riding on a zenzen or in a bumpy cart. She was feeling the bruises from yesterday's intense wippen game.

"Careful up ahead," Durgen warned. "You will need some height for the—"

"I see it," Kasha replied. They were approaching the outskirts of the city. Trees were taller here, and beyond them, she remembered, were craggy mountains. She'd need to fly between crevices to go east. The gaps in the rock face weren't all that easy to find.

The gig's nose suddenly rose sharply, pressing Kasha and Durgen back into their seats. Kasha brought it level again, and they easily cleared the treetops.

"A slow climb is a preferable technique," Durgen said.

"But this is more fun!" Kasha said. Actually, she had thought she *was* guiding the gig into a slow climb. It was harder to control than she'd realized.

"So, with the crevice . . . ," she said. She peered ahead trying to spot the entrance. All she could see was rock.

"I thought you knew all about piloting," Durgen said with a smirk.

"I thought you would want to participate," Kasha said. "I know how much you hate being bored. Besides," she added, slowing down the gig, afraid she'd miss the entrance and crash into the boulders, "if the copilot does nothing, he's just dead weight. Right?"

"Drop slightly," Durgen instructed with a grin. "But be ready to go into fast turns. You'll need to adjust the angles on the control panel."

Kasha nodded. She was glad she wasn't doing this run on her own. She vowed to put in more hours on gig duty.

"Here's the entrance," Durgen said. "Get ready!"

Kasha peered ahead, knowing that she was going to have to use fast reflexes to do the subtle shifting maneuvers required to make it through the crevice. Her paw hovered over the control panel, ready to start the first of the quick turns.

Now!

She turned the control, then reached across the control board to grab the other. Her paw knocked the throttle and the gig suddenly lurched forward. She'd thrown the gig into high speed!

"Slow down!" Durgen cried.

"I can't!" Kasha said. She couldn't risk taking her paws off the controls or the joystick. She worked the switches and the gig responded instantly, shifting left and right, tilting, rounding sharp corners, all at a breakneck speed.

Kasha's heart pounded hard in her furred chest. She sensed Durgen's tension but pushed it out of her thoughts. All she could focus on was the next move. Otherwise the gig would crash into the side of the cliffs. She wasn't going to let that happen.

Durgen must have known she needed every ounce of concentration. He didn't say a word.

They burst out of the crevice on the other side of the mountain.

She'd made it!

She grabbed the throttle and pulled back to slow down. The gig smoothly coasted over a beautiful clearing.

"Well," Durgen said shakily. "We certainly made this run in record time."

Kasha nodded. She was too wound up to speak.

"That wippen game is doing wonders for your reflexes," Durgen commented.

"I had just been thinking that yesterday," Kasha said. "That foraging and playing wippen use a lot of the same skills."

"There should be a foraging group around here," Durgen said, peering at the landscape below. "They went out very early this morning."

She gazed down at the landscape, trying to pick out the foragers in the fields. She had never harvested this far from Leeandra. It was unfamiliar terrain. Rocks loomed over the group, which was ringed on one side by boulders and a river on the other.

She watched the forage, fascinated by how it looked from the air. The klees stood around the cart, chatting. The gars worked hard, picking and hauling the crop. The klees barely paid attention to them, other than to occasionally jab them with sticks to make them move faster. She was surprised how small the group of klees looked, in among the towering stalks, surrounded by even larger trees. How could the gars be used as protection? she wondered. They looked so weak and defenseless.

"They're almost done," Durgen commented. "They'll turn around soon."

A flash of movement caught Kasha's eye, and she looked over to see a tang leap down from a rock. Kasha gasped—she'd never even seen it coming! Its bright green body blended with the foliage.

"The tang!" Kasha cried as it crept up to the edge of the field. "They don't know it's there! We have to help them."

She hit the controls and the gig tipped its nose down. Durgen placed his paw firmly over hers. "No," he said. "They have to handle it on their own."

"But—"

"This is a scouting assignment—we have no weapons," Durgen reminded her.

"We must alert them!"

"The tang will attack the gars—that will certainly alert the klees!"

Kasha gaped at him, then looked away. *What's wrong with me*? Gars had always been used as the first line of defense.

The tang made its move, leaping onto an unsuspecting gar. The gar let out an agonized howl, and just as Durgen predicted, this sent the klees into action. They quickly loaded what they could into the cart and took off.

Leaving the gars behind.

Kasha's eyes widened. "They're just abandoning them."

Durgen looked at her, perplexed. "They have to get the harvest back. The gars will take care of themselves."

"But—" Kasha stopped herself. Once again she was arguing against a practice she'd accepted all her life. Durgen would think she was crazy.

She shook her head. *It's all that talk of my father's last night*, she told herself.

She glanced down below again. The gars were racing away from the area, stumbling over one another, tripping in their haste over rocks, stumps. The tang stood, the captured gar still struggling under its talons on the ground, whimpering, screaming.

The terror of the gars reached all the way up to the gig, up into Kasha's bones. She could feel it. Taste it. She'd felt that same fear herself during a tang attack, desperate to escape, frantic to save her colleagues, her friends.

She had never realized that the gars felt the same way. Of course, she knew they were afraid to die or to feel pain, but today she saw something different.

Today she saw the similarities between the gars and the klees.

Not possible. Ridiculous. That's like saying just because my zenzen gets hungry or resists a command, it is just like me because I get hungry and disobey orders from Durgen. We are not the same. They are—

"You're right," she declared to Durgen. "There is nothing we can do for them. We should get on our way."

"Travel northeast. I will let you know when it is time to change direction."

"Got it." Kasha adjusted the controls. She pulled back hard on the throttle and the gig rocketed away, the screams of the gar growing faint behind them.

SEVEN

This is the big one!" Coach Jorsa declared. "This game determines who wins the championship. It's now or never!" She strode back and forth in front of the Blue Team klees.

"Give it your all!" she continued. "Keep the gars working for you; remember to pay attention to one another. Claws in, but play hard. You know the Red Team will."

"Kasha is our secret weapon!" someone piped up. "The way she played last game—"

"Not so secret," Jorsa interrupted. "The other team will be going after her and going after her hard."

"I'm ready," Kasha said. She tossed her scoop from one paw to the other, eager to get started. She glanced at Boon and he gave her a huge grin. *I may be hungry for a win*, she thought, *but Boon is ravenous for it*.

"All right, Blue Team!" Jorsa shouted. "Mount your zenzens!"

The Blue Team klees roared together, then bounded toward the corral.

"We really have a shot!" Boon said. He paced on all fours as he and Kasha waited their turn to get their zenzens. If all that excitement could be harnessed, Boon would have powered a gig with his energy.

"I've never made it to the final games before! And it's all thanks to you!"

"The whole team," Kasha said. "We play well together."

"Especially you and me," Boon said.

Kasha grinned. "That's true."

The two teams trotted into the stadium to the sound of cheering. Klees waved red and blue banners, and Kasha could see that every seat was filled. The day was bright and crisp—perfect weather for wippen.

Gars ran out onto the field as klees barked orders at them to herd them into their opening positions.

Is it hard for them to get back out to play after last week's death? she wondered. Then the game master sent the ball into play, and Kasha brought her full attention to the field.

The ball moved fast, Jorsa was right. The Red Team played hard, and no matter where Kasha rode, at least one Red Team klee and several gars were right there with her.

Boon got hold of the ball, and Kasha could see he was using the technique she'd employed last week. He kept throwing the ball to gars, even when they were behind the lines or off to the side. But the Red Team wasn't surprised by this tactic—instead they kept their gars near the goals, knowing that at some point a klee would try to score. They successfully blocked three attempts by the Blue Team to get the ball into the goal.

We have to try something else, Kasha thought. *But what?*

Stick to the simple approach, she decided. Get the ball and get it into the goal.

"Open!" she cried, as once again Boon had the ball. He hurled it to her. A Red Team klee galloped straight at her, trying to intercept, but Kasha was too quick. She scooped the ball into her net.

A Red Team gar leaped up and tried to knock her scoop. She held it out of his reach and kicked her zenzen into a fast trot. The gar stumbled and fell.

Kasha's heart froze. Did her zenzen trample the downed gar?

She turned to check, and in that moment, another gar grabbed for the ball. She whipped around and snatched it back, scratching his hand with her claws. He let out a yelp of pain and released the ball.

Focus! she admonished herself. *The gars aren't your concern. Winning the game is all that you should be thinking about.*

A Red Team klee bore down on her, and she tossed the ball to a gar. She had to get her mind back in the game.

To regain her concentration she rode her zenzen around the perimeter of the field. She needed to feel at one with her mount, and in synch with the team. As she trotted along the outskirts of the field, the Red Team made another score. The Blue Team was behind.

Okay, she was ready. She hunkered down into the saddle and charged straight at the Red Team klee who had possession of the ball. The klee threw it to a gar, who raced away.

"Get it!" Kasha snarled at one of her gars. "And get it to me!"

The gar dashed after the ball, darting in and out among the snorting zenzens. Again, Kasha felt a chill as she watched the gar's progress through the crowded field. She squirmed as the gar she'd sent after the ball was knocked aside by a Red Team player, the klee's scoop hitting the gar hard. The gar fell, and was sent off the field.

As another gar came to take his place, Kasha's eyes swept over the gar holding pen.

They look so small, she thought. *And afraid.*

The klees might call the wippen gars "players," but this was no game to them. They weren't having fun. They weren't overjoyed by victory, excited to be competing, disappointed with defeat, and eager to prove themselves the next time. They hated this game. They just didn't have a choice.

Her father was right. Foraging was an activity vital to the survival of all—gars and klees alike. Klees and gars equally faced danger every time they went out to the fields for the good of Leeandra.

But wippen was a game, a sport—an entertainment for those who watched and an exhilarating competition for those who participated. *Those* klees *who participated*, Kasha corrected herself. It was unfair to expect gars to feel the same way.

Someone threw Kasha the ball and she fumbled, dropping it. One of the Blue Team gars retrieved it for her, but it was too late. A Red Team player easily snatched it away from her. And made another goal.

The Blue Team was behind.

The horn blew—it was time for the break.

The Blue Team headed for the break area. The crackling energy they'd all shared at the start of the game had evaporated. Even the zenzens seemed defeated.

Coach Jorsa approached Kasha, a look of concern on her face. "Do I need to take you out?" she asked. "You seem to be hesitating. Do you have injuries from last week? You played very hard. It would be no dishonor."

"I'm fine," Kasha said. How could she explain to the coach that she couldn't see the game the same way anymore? She wanted to win, she wanted the team to be proud and victorious. But for some reason she just couldn't do it at the expense of the gars.

Boon slumped beside her. "Well, at least we got this close," he said with a sad smile. "That's better than nothing, I guess."

Kasha looked at her friend's disappointed face and felt a flash of defiance. "Don't count us out yet," she told him.

I will get this team to victory, Kasha vowed. For Boon. For them all.

Now she just had to figure out a way to do it without putting any gars in danger.

EiGHt

It's not over yet," Coach Jorsa told the disheartened Blue Team. "If you go out there thinking you have already lost, then you definitely will. So if there's anyone feeling that way, dismount and I'll put someone else in!"

All of the klees glanced at one another, wondering if anyone would take themselves out of the game.

Kasha stared down at her zenzen, not wanting to catch anyone's eyes. *Can I really do this?* she asked herself. Could she avoid using the gars? Or would that guarantee that the team would lose? That wouldn't be fair either.

She just couldn't bring herself to abandon the game. She'd come so far—and she knew she was one of the strongest players.

But was she strong enough to score without gars?

She was determined to try.

"All right then!" Coach Jorsa declared. "If you're staying in, then you're committed to win!"

The Blue Team klees let out a group roar and charged

back out onto the field, fired up and ready to play. Gars from both teams scattered across the turf, ready to move quickly.

Kasha took a breath. She'd given herself an impossible task. Simply being on the field put gars at risk. Everywhere she looked there were dangers: fast-moving zenzens and determined klees wielding powerful scoops.

Yet if she avoided the ball, she'd lose the game. Maybe she should just play guard? Keep the klees from scoring?

"Kasha. Face-off!" Coach Jorsa shouted.

There went the "guard only" plan.

Kasha trotted to the center of the field. This time her opponent was a large black-and-white-spotted klee. Gars surrounded them, ready to follow klee orders to catch or steal the ball.

This is stupid, she thought. *Just play the way you always play. With or without gars, go for the goal.*

The game master tossed the ball into play, and Kasha lunged for it. The ball landed neatly in her net and the game was on.

Kasha kicked her zenzen and took off. She swerved to avoid the gars surrounding her, trying to block and distract her. Who was open? She scanned the field. There weren't any gars around Boon. She hurled the ball in his direction.

The ball whizzed by him, as Kasha watched in dismay. How could he have missed the pass? Then she realized—the reason he'd been open was that he wasn't in a good position, so he hadn't been expecting the ball.

Red Team and Blue Team gars raced over and flung

themselves onto the ball. Kasha winced. The pileups were another way gars were injured—just the kind of thing she was trying to avoid.

A Red Team gar emerged from the pile with the ball. Boon galloped to him and used the handle of his scoop to try to knock the ball away, while a Red Team klee rode up to defend. The gar looked panicked.

"Here!" Kasha screamed. "Throw it to me!"

Without thinking, the gar flung the ball to Kasha. She was as startled as the other players and nearly missed the catch. In the heat of the moment, the gar had simply followed a klee order.

As soon as the ball left his hands he must have realized his mistake—he raced toward her. But Kasha dug her heels into her zenzen's sides and loped toward the goal.

Gars scrambled to block her but she made it all the way—to score!

Scoring the first goal in this half energized her teammates. Their determination seemed to renew as the ball went back into play.

As the game continued, both teams played aggressively. Kasha watched disheartened as several injured gars were removed from play. She hadn't harmed a single one of them herself, but for the first time in her life, the sight sickened her.

The game was close now. Once again the Blue Team had a shot at winning the championship. Kasha wanted that win as badly as her teammates; she could taste the sweetness of the victory as strongly as she could smell the mud spatters on her fur. But she just wouldn't put the gars at risk. As they neared the end of the game, that was getting more and more difficult. Both teams were rigorously defending their positions.

But how? *Keep them out of the line of fire somehow.*

The Red Team would expect her to play the standard strategies. Maybe she could win by confusing them. It had worked before—like in the game when she had only passed to gars. Could it work again by *never* passing to them?

She gained control of the ball. Time to put her plan into action. She whistled for Blue Team gars. As she loped back and forth across the field, never approaching the goal, the gars dashed over to her.

"Cover Boon!" she ordered them. "Go!"

The gars raced to the other side of the field. Boon prepared for the pass.

It never came.

The Red Team saw the gars heading for Boon. They sent their own gars after them. That gave Kasha the opening she was hoping for.

"Yah!" she shrieked. She leaned far forward in her saddle and roared into the zenzen's ears. The zenzen galloped fast across the field.

By the time the Red Team realized they'd been sent in the wrong direction, it was too late. Kasha was close enough to the goal to throw.

She stood in her stirrups and flung the ball hard. She squeezed her eyes tight, terrified she'd missed the shot.

A cheer went up—she'd scored!

And won the game!

Kasha's eyes blinked open. The Blue Team went wild.

Boon let out a roar and yanked on his reins so that his zenzen reared up and whinnied. Players tossed their scoops into the air while the crowd applauded. Coach Jorsa mounted and rode out onto the field to join her team in the victory circle around the stadium.

Kasha's breath slowly returned to normal as she trotted around the arena. She pulled her zenzen to a stop for the trophy ceremony. Jorsa accepted the prize on behalf of the team, praising them all.

"We did it!" Boon beamed beside her. "I mean, *you* did it!"

"I—I can't take any credit," Kasha said.

She flicked the reins and followed the rest of her team off the field. She felt dazed. She couldn't shake the feeling that she was out of place, an imposter. Her teammates were jubilant and all she felt was . . . confused.

"You are a truly talented player, Kasha," Coach Jorsa said as Kasha dismounted. "Each game you used a different technique to keep the Red Team off kilter."

"Yes . . . ," Kasha said. "I guess I did." She gave her zenzen water to drink and lapped up some herself.

"Brilliant strategy," Jorsa continued. "By avoiding the gars entirely the Red Team couldn't predict your moves. We will have to remember that for next year."

"Truly," Boon chimed in. "How did you think of that?"

Kasha dropped to all fours for a long stretch. How could she answer? They would never understand that she couldn't bring herself to harm the gars. They would think she was crazy. As crazy as she feared her own father might be.

"I knew we would have a better chance if we stayed unpredictable," she finally said.

"Your hunch paid off," Jorsa said. "See you at the victory feast!" Jorsa left Kasha and Boon and went to congratulate the other players.

Victory feast. Kasha stood back up. "I—I think I'm going to skip the feast."

Boon stared at her. "But the feast is the best part of winning!"

"I'm too tired, and I think I may have pulled a muscle," Kasha said.

"Oh! Do you want me to—"

Kasha cut him off. "No! You should go! You've worked hard for this. You have waited three seasons for this honor."

"If you're really sure . . . ," Boon said.

Kasha smiled. "I'm going to go to my father's. He and I have some things to talk about."

She watched as Boon walked his zenzen to the corral and then joined the other celebrating players.

What is wrong with me? she wondered as she brought her zenzen to the corral. She strode out of the arena and headed toward the monorail. She noticed several gars being led by some klees, and as they walked by, she studied them. Here, out of the arena, she felt nothing for the inferior creatures. She felt no need to protect them, saw them simply as they were—animals that served many purposes in the klee community.

You took an absurd risk, she admonished herself. *Your misguided concern for the gars nearly cost the championship*. It must have been all that talk of her father's. It had sent her down the wrong path.

She abruptly turned around. She wouldn't have dinner with Seegen tonight. And, she promised herself, she would not be compromised by misplaced compassion for the gars again.

Not now. Not ever.

And yet . . .

She strode past the arena and stopped. She stared up at the high walls.

Wippen mattered a lot to Boon. She wouldn't want to take that away from him.

But that didn't mean she had to keep playing.

The next season is a long way away, she told herself. *Plenty of time to decide.*

To decide many things.

GUNNY

PROLOGUE

Jeffrey Wright paced in a tight pattern, jingling the spare change in his pocket. The room was dark. Marvin Halliday's jazz club, the Blue Moon, was still being built, and the light fixtures weren't installed yet. The late afternoon sun cast dark shadows around the two men.

"We've got to do something," Jeffrey told Marvin. "I can't take the pressure anymore. And if you won't help me, then I'll do it myself."

"Yeah?" a voice snarled behind Jeffrey. "You and what army?"

Jeffrey froze. He knew that voice. For a moment Marvin and Jeffrey locked eyes, sharing the same terrified look. Slowly—so that the goon behind him would know that he wasn't about to try anything—Jeffrey turned.

There were three of them. All big. All smiling. Without a word, one guy took a sledgehammer and smashed a deep hole into the nearby painted pillar. Another knocked over a table, taking several chairs down with it.

Then there was the third guy, grinning.

Why is he just standing there? Jeffrey wondered. For one second Jeffrey didn't understand what the sudden, searing pain in his arm was. Somehow he felt the bullet tearing into his flesh before he heard the gun go off.

From far away—so far away—Jeffrey heard Marvin shouting, and some crashing, and *pop! pop! pop!*

Jeffrey flung himself to the floor behind the toppled table. A volley of bullets ripped through it, splintered wood and paint chips raining down on him.

Someone's got to hear this, he thought. *Someone's got to come in and stop it!* He crawled toward the bar, desperate for cover.

There was a *crash* and glass flew everywhere. *The window. Did they just throw Marvin out his own window?*

Crawling was too slow. Jeffrey pulled himself up to a low crouch, clutching his burning left arm. The kitchen door was within reach. From there he'd run out the back. They wouldn't gun him down in the street.

Of course they wouldn't. Not when they could put his lights out forever right here.

Jeffrey fell forward, his chest thrust outward from the impact of the bullets in his back. He went down, his face smashing into the rubble strewn over the floor.

He thought he could hear his breath, ragged and full of pain. It sounded like a roar in his ears, like the ocean. Or maybe that was the sound of his blood rushing out of him.

Something landed near his face. A gun, still smoking. That was the last thing he ever saw.

ONE

"Night, Gunny!"

Vincent "Gunny" Van Dyke waved good-bye without turning around as he walked through the bustling kitchen of the Manhattan Tower Hotel. His bellman's shift was over and he was looking forward to the weekend.

The new kid he had just hired—"Dodger" was it?—opened the back door with a flourish and a little bow. "Evening, sir," Dodger said with a grin.

"Good night, my good man," Gunny replied, sounding as high class as one of the big shots who often stayed at the hotel.

Dodger gave Gunny a once-over. "You look swank," he said with his thick Brooklyn accent. "Got plans?"

"You bet I do," Gunny replied.

Dodger snapped his fingers. "You're off to hear your friend's band up in Harlem!" Dodger clutched Gunny's wide lapels as if he were a man begging for his life. "Please, you gotta take me with you."

"No can do, Dodger," Gunny said. "You're on the night shift now."

Dodger mimed stabbing himself in the chest. "Cut out my heart, why don'tcha," he moaned.

Gunny laughed. He liked the squirt. He was rough around the edges maybe, but solid.

"Don't worry, Dodger," Gunny promised. "Once you're back on days, I'll bring you up to Chubby Malloy's Paradise to hear Jumpin' Jed and the JiveMasters."

"Will you get me a girl, too?" Dodger asked eagerly.

Gunny laughed again. "I'm not a miracle worker."

"Cruel." Dodger took a step backward and looked stricken. "So cruel." Then he smirked and winked.

The sun was dipping low, and the chill in the air made Gunny walk briskly to the subway. He put his nickel in the slot and hurried down the stairs for the long trip uptown to Harlem.

Gunny peered out the window as the subway crawled out of the tunnel and rumbled along the elevated tracks. *We go back a long ways, ol' Jed and me.*

Jed was a bit older than Gunny and they had known each other since childhood in Virginia. After the Great War, they both moved up to New York. Now, almost twenty years later, Jumpin' Jed was the leader of his own band at the nicest nightclub in Harlem—maybe all of New York City—and Gunny was bell captain at the Manhattan Tower Hotel. *We've done well for ourselves,* Gunny thought with satisfaction.

Still, something nagged at him. Gunny didn't crave the flash of Jumpin' Jed's life as an entertainer. But sometimes he wondered if there were something more he should be doing, something just outside view that he was meant to discover.

The clattering train pulled into Gunny's stop with a screech. This neighborhood was a lot noisier than the fancy area around the hotel. Here pushcart peddlers shouted out to customers, men and women hurried home from work, children played stickball in the street while neighbors hung out windows and yelled down to them.

When Gunny turned onto Jed's block, the roar of construction sounds added to the din. He stopped to check out the new building going up. A group of small boys huddled around the work site, watching in awe as a crane hoisted supplies to the upper stories.

"It's going to be a while yet before it's done," a man beside Gunny commented. "Ambrose Jackson is doing mighty well for himself."

"Hope he'll have some tenants for all those new office spaces," Gunny said, watching in fascination as several workmen walked expertly along girders high above him. "Must be a real optimist."

Despite the Depression still raging around them, Ambrose Jackson managed to acquire properties. Ambrose didn't live in the neighborhood, but everyone seemed to know him anyway.

How does he do it? Gunny wondered. So many people were struggling, but Jackson kept starting new enterprises.

Gunny turned to go. Suddenly he was body-slammed so hard the breath was knocked out of him. He flung out his hands and grabbed on to the person who had rammed into him, trying to steady himself. He looked into the very angry face of Jeffrey Wright Jr.

"Junior!" Gunny exclaimed. "Where's the fire?" Junior was the sixteen-year-old son of Jeffrey Wright Sr., the drummer in Jumpin' Jed's band. Gunny had known the boy for years. Junior was the spitting image of his father, with his short dark hair, almond-shaped eyes, and deep cocoa skin. His eleven-year-old sister, Delia, looked more like her mother.

"Let go of me, old man!" Junior wriggled out of Gunny's grip and tore down the sidewalk.

Gunny glared after Junior as he vanished into the crowd. "Flighty kid," Gunny grumbled. "No respect."

"Junior!" a woman called. "Junior Wright, you get back here this instant!"

Gunny turned and saw Mrs. Wright standing with Delia.

"Evening, Mrs. Wright, Delia," Gunny said as he approached them. "I see Junior is in a lather over something."

Mrs. Wright had a hand on her hip and a frown on her face. "I'm so sorry, Gunny," she said, embarrassment coloring her dark cheeks. "He shouldn't behave like that."

"It's the age," Gunny said. "With luck, he'll outgrow it."

Mrs. Wright laughed. "I hope Delia never grows *into* it then!"

"Mama." Delia rolled her dark brown eyes.

"What has him so fussed?" Gunny asked.

Mrs. Wright sighed. "He and his father had a fight."

"Again," Delia added.

Mrs. Wright gave the girl a warning look, as if she didn't want family business to be so public. Then, changing the subject, she asked, "What brings you uptown?"

"I'm here to see Jed Sweeney, upstairs."

"Oh, you missed him," Mrs. Wright said.

That surprised Gunny. Jed was expecting him. "Do you know where he went?"

"Try Marvin Halliday's place," Mrs. Wright suggested. "He was going that way."

"I'll do that," Gunny said.

Is Jed checking up on the competition? Gunny wondered as he headed toward the still-under-construction nightclub. The whole neighborhood was abuzz about Halliday building a rival club just a few blocks from Chubby Malloy's Paradise.

As soon as Gunny rounded the corner he knew something was wrong.

The street was deserted. He had never seen a block so empty in Harlem—not ever.

He moved forward slowly, his eyes scanning for an explanation for the uncommon stillness. During the Great War Gunny had learned silence could be a warning sign of something deadly—a trap, a recent slaughter.

As he got closer, he saw shattered glass all over the sidewalk. The Blue Moon's front window was smashed.

Not good.

His feet made crunching sounds as he crossed to the door. Standing to one side, his back against the wall of the building, he tapped the door lightly. It swung open easily. No response from inside. He cautiously stepped into the dark bar.

Even in the dim light it was obvious the club had been wrecked.

And worst of all . . .

He could see the dead body on the floor.

Two

Gunny froze. He wasn't alone.

His body reflexively crouched into a defensive stance, hands up, ready to move in any direction. When his eyes finally adjusted to the dark, his blood ran cold.

He was staring at the barrel of a gun.

Guns. He hated the things. They filled him with rage, yet he was helpless before them. He had found that out soon enough when he enlisted in the army. He had believed in that fight and wanted to put his life on the line for his country and for freedom. But then came basic training.

"Van Dyke, you're up," the sergeant barked.

"Yes, sir!" Gunny took the proffered rifle, lifted it, placed it in exactly the right position. Then . . .

Nothing.

He looked through the site. Had a perfect bead on the target. He took a deep breath.

Nothing. He just couldn't pull the trigger.

The men had teased him about it for days. He knew

they were joking and meant no harm, but it still stung. One of them called him "Gunny," in the ironic way the hulking Private McCall was nicknamed "Tiny." Everywhere he went that week, all he heard was men calling out "Gunny! Hey, Gunny!"

"*Gunny.*"

Gunny roused himself. Someone was actually saying his name. Here and now. He peeled his eyes away from the gun barrel and allowed his gaze to travel up to the face above it.

"Jed!" Gunny looked back down at the body on the floor. It wasn't Marvin Halliday, as he had expected. It was Jeffrey Wright Sr.

Gunny couldn't believe what he was seeing. Jumpin' Jed holding a gun over the dead body of his own drummer.

"Jed, what happened here?" Gunny asked.

Jed seemed stunned. He stared down at Jeffrey. "I don't know—"

"Hands in the air!" a voice behind Gunny shouted. "Now!"

Jed looked past Gunny, then at the gun, as if he just realized he was holding it. He dropped it with a clatter to the floor and raised his hands.

As Gunny turned around, cops swarmed into the demolished nightclub.

A short, squat policeman roughly grabbed Jed's wrists, yanked them behind his back, and handcuffed him.

"I didn't do anything!" Jed protested.

"If you're arresting him, why aren't you arresting me too?" Gunny demanded. "I'm standing right here!"

"Don't tempt us," the policeman said.

A thin detective with hawklike features stepped forward carefully. "We saw you walk in just a minute ago. Not enough time to do all this." He gestured at the room, then his beady eyes returned to Jed. "Besides, *he* was holding the weapon."

"I just found him like this," Jed said. "Jeffrey Wright is a member of my band—and my friend! Why would I want to kill him?"

"So *that's* Jeffrey Wright," a fresh-faced blond cop said.

"You know him?" Gunny asked, surprised.

"We hear the same rumors everyone else does," the officer holding Jed said. "And what we've been hearing is that Jeffrey Wright wanted to strike out on his own. Start his own band."

The hawk-faced detective bent down and, with a handkerchief, gingerly picked up the gun Jed had just dropped. "Here's my theory, fellas," he declared loudly as he stood. "Jumpin' Jed followed Wright to a meeting with Marvin Halliday to try to persuade his drummer not to defect." He glanced at Jed and smirked. "I guess the meeting got ugly."

"That's crazy," Jed protested. "I came to tell Jeffrey if he wanted to leave there'd be no hard feelings."

"Sure you did," the detective said.

The hawklike detective suddenly stepped right up to Jed. "What did you do with Marvin Halliday?" he bellowed inches from Jed's face.

"Nothing!" Jed said. "I never even saw him."

The detective looked Jed up and down. "Bring

him in, boys. We'll ask him more questions at the precinct."

"Don't worry, Jed," Gunny shouted as the cops roughly hauled Jed away. "I'll get you out of this!"

He just had to figure out how.

THREE

Gunny stepped out into the street, now packed with people.

"Why are you taking Jed?" someone in the crowd hollered.

"Where's Marvin?"

The cops ignored the crowd and shoved Jed into the back of the police wagon. Men and women were forced to disperse as the wagon eased through the crowd.

"What's going on?" someone shouted. All eyes turned to Gunny.

Gunny cleared his throat. "As you can all see, someone destroyed Marvin Halliday's club," he announced. He took a deep breath. "Jeffrey Wright has been shot. That's what Jed has been arrested for."

"No!" a man hollered.

"They think Jed did it? He loved Jeffrey like he was his own brother!" a woman near Gunny declared.

The man Gunny had spoken to at the construction site earlier pushed forward. "You know who did this!

Chubby Malloy! He doesn't want anything to compete with his Paradise."

Another clear voice rang out. "I heard Chubby threaten Marvin!"

The crowd parted and Gunny saw that Ambrose Jackson was the speaker. He stepped forward, his slick suit contrasting with the shabbier clothes of the neighborhood folk.

"I heard Chubby swear that no new club would open up in Harlem while he was around," Ambrose said.

The mutters and murmurs turned into a rumble, then a roar. "Let's go get Chubby!"

This was quickly turning into a mob scene. And mobs were always dangerous.

Gunny had to stop this. He knew it was possible that all this had happened on Chubby's orders. But violence wasn't the solution.

"Stop!" he shouted. Even at the top of his lungs, no one could hear him.

Glancing around, he grabbed a garbage can. Luckily, it was empty. He flipped it over and clambered on top of it. "Stop! Now!" he hollered.

He knew he looked like a crazy person, shouting and flailing his arms from the top of a garbage can, but he didn't care. If it helped stop this tide of fury, then so be it.

"Stop! I mean it!"

The shouts and rumbles died down and the men and women stared at Gunny.

"We can't meet violence with violence," Gunny declared. "We may believe Chubby was behind this, but we don't know for sure. We're acting just like those cops who took Jed away. We have nothing but what they call 'circumstantial evidence.' Besides," he added, pausing so he could meet the eyes of as many people as he could, "I know for a fact that Chubby has been good to a lot of you. He employs folks right here in this crowd, and he's Jed's boss."

He let those words sink in. Several people gazed shamefacedly down at the ground, others shoved their hands in their pockets and shifted their weight from side to side or whispered to one another.

"Our first thoughts have to go out to Mrs. Wright and her children," Gunny told them. "She's going to need us, and we can't help her and her family if we're all locked up for rioting."

That settled them down once and for all. Gunny spotted in the crowd a plump, older woman everyone called "Cousin Mary." "Cousin Mary. Can you and a few of the women go to Mrs. Wright? She shouldn't be alone when she gets the news."

"Of course, Gunny," Cousin Mary said.

The crowd dispersed and Gunny climbed back down from the garbage can. He mopped his brow with shaking hands. He had no idea he'd been so nervous.

At least I can tell Jed he has the full support of the neighborhood, Gunny thought as he headed for the police station.

It was a chaotic scene inside the station, and he had to shout to make himself heard by the desk sergeant. When he asked for Jed, the thick-necked officer grunted and aimed a stubby thumb toward a set of doors. "Still in holding," the officer said.

A skinny red-haired man stood in Jed's cell cradling a sheaf of papers. "It isn't looking good, Mr. Sweeney," he was saying as Gunny walked up to the cell. "Perhaps you should consider a plea."

"Perhaps you should consider another line of work!" Gunny said angrily.

Startled, the guy lost his grip on his papers, and they flew out of his hands. He bent down to pick them up, looking disgusted that he had to touch the filthy jail-cell floor.

"I'm innocent, and I'm not going to say any different," Jed told the man who was obviously his lawyer.

"You got that right," Gunny agreed.

The man stood and faced Gunny. Gunny took in the bright blue eyes behind skinny glasses, the acne-pocked skin, and the unruly red hair. "Are you old enough to be an attorney?" Gunny asked.

Jed laughed, and the man flushed deep scarlet, almost as red as his hair. "This may be my first case, but that doesn't mean—"

"We're getting you a new lawyer," Gunny told Jed. "A grown-up one."

"Just because I'm young—"

"Now, Gunny," Jed said, "let's give young Mr. Gordon a chance."

"Have they set bail?" Gunny asked.

"They set it very high," the lawyer admitted. "Mr. Sweeney had motive, and they did find him with the murder weapon. And without any witnesses . . ."

"What about other suspects?" Gunny demanded.

"I'm sure the police are investigating every lead," Mr. Gordon said.

"Really?" Gunny scoffed. "Why should they when you're already offering Jed to them on a platter with this plea agreement."

Mr. Gordon had nothing to say to that. He straightened to his full height—which seemed even taller because he was so skinny—spun around, and left the cell.

Gunny looked at Jed. Although he was around ten years older than Gunny, Gunny had never noticed Jed's age. Until now. Here in the jail cell, his seventy-odd years seemed etched in the lines of Jed's dark face. His white hair added to the impression of an elderly man.

"How's the Wright family?" Jed asked.

"Cousin Mary went to sit with them," Gunny said. "And the whole neighborhood believes you're innocent. Things got kind of crazy after the cops hauled you away."

"What do you mean?"

"People were fired up—wanted to go smash up the Paradise. It nearly turned into a riot."

Jed let out a low whistle. "Not good."

"I managed to quiet things down before they really got out of hand," Gunny said.

"Did you, now?" Jed looked at Gunny thoughtfully. "I've always known you were a born leader."

Gunny laughed. "Maybe *you* knew. It was news to me today!"

Jed twisted his ring. He'd worn that ring for as long as Gunny could remember.

"Listen, there's something I need you to do," Jed said.

"Anything," Gunny replied.

"Keep an eye on Junior Wright. Mrs. Wright is going to have her hands full. Jeffrey watched over them during the day while she was at work. Now there's no one to do that. Delia is a sweet kid with lots of activities that keep her out of trouble. But Junior . . ."

"I don't know how to take care of a teenage boy!" Gunny protested. "What am I supposed to do?"

"Learn quickly," Jed said.

FOUR

Gunny raised his eyebrow. "Not funny."

"You're right. It's not," Jed said. "This is important. For Junior. And for you."

"I have nothing to offer a kid. And seriously, Jed," Gunny added, "what can a kid do for me—other than annoy me?"

"Promise me," Jed said.

"But—"

Jed reached through the bars and placed his hands on Gunny's shoulders. "This matters more to me than getting the bail or even helping to free me. Just trust me. It's important that you watch over him."

Gunny stared at his old friend. In the past Jed had pushed Gunny toward trying things he didn't really want to do. Somehow it always turned out right—or at least, not too badly wrong. Jed's grave expression made it very clear that he was sincere, and that this was a very big deal.

"I still don't see why you think this is something that I'd be good for, but all right. I promise."

"You underestimate yourself," Jed said. Then he grinned. "I won't say you'll never regret it," he joked. "But I will say it will give you something you'll need."

"If you say so," Gunny said skeptically. "The faster I get you out on bail, the quicker *you* can take on Junior. So I'm going to get right on it."

Gunny left the jail, not sure what his next move should be. *Home*, he decided. He'd be able to think better there. Make some plans.

He stepped off the curb. The squeal of tires on pavement made him look up. A shiny black car was taking the turn at breakneck speed, hugging the street so tight, one wheel jumped the pavement.

Gunny flung himself forward, trying to make it as far across the street as possible. He stumbled, but didn't go down. He whirled around to see the car barreling toward him. The car sped by him, missing him by mere inches.

But it didn't move so fast that he couldn't see the driver.

Junior Wright.

Gunny gaped after the speeding car. *What is that fool child doing out joyriding in a fancy car like that?* And whose car was the kid driving? Could Junior have *stolen* it? Another thought hit Gunny, hard—did Junior know about his dad?

Gunny dashed after the car like a sprinter a third his age.

Well, look at that, Gunny thought as the black car screeched to a sudden stop at the red light. *Nice to see Junior didn't break that particular traffic law!*

Before the light could change, Gunny yanked open the car door.

Junior's head whipped around to face Gunny. "What the—" he blurted out.

Gunny slammed the door shut.

"You can't just jump into my car!" Junior shouted.

"I just did. You can't run me over in the street. And what do you mean, *your* car?"

Horns blared behind them as the light changed, and Junior hit the gas.

"I got the car from Ambrose Jackson."

"Why would Ambrose give you a car?" Gunny clutched the car handle so he wouldn't slip around on the seat. Junior had slowed down, but he wove in and out of traffic like a football player avoiding being tackled.

"He didn't *give* it to me," Junior said as if Gunny were an idiot missing the obvious. "He loaned it to me so I could do errands for him."

"What kind of errands?"

"Easy ones. I just have to pick up envelopes from people around town."

Gunny's eyes stayed on the road, trying to will the cars to part for them. "Envelopes?" Gunny repeated.

"Ambrose is great, man," Junior continued. "He even introduced me to the owner of Duke's Gym so I can work on my boxing."

Gunny's eyebrow shot up. "Boxing? I never heard anything about you training as a boxer."

Junior snorted. "That's because everyone is set against it. My father practically outlawed even *talking* about it in our house. But not Ambrose. He believes in me." His dark expression grew darker. "More than my own father. All my dad does is give me grief."

Gunny felt his heart sink. Right. His dad.

Gunny slid his arm across the seat behind Junior. "Listen, Junior, something serious has happened. Park the car and come with me."

That got Junior's attention. "What happened?" he demanded.

Before Gunny could answer, shots rang out.

Gunny swiveled in his seat just in time to see the bullets take out their taillights.

Someone was shooting at *them*!

FIVE

Junior yelped and flung his hands up to cover his head. The car swerved toward the oncoming traffic.

"Junior!" Gunny reached over the boy to grab the wheel. "Keep shifting!" he shouted, since Junior had access to the clutch and manual gear shift.

A siren wailed. Gunny desperately hoped it was the police.

Ping! A bullet hit the rearview mirror, shearing it off.

"They're going to kill us!" Junior wailed.

Gunny's heart leaped into his throat, plummeted to his stomach and came back up again. The sirens weren't from police cars—they announced the fire engine heading straight toward them.

He yanked the wheel hard, his elbow connecting with some part of Junior. The car swerved sharply and squeaked out of the fire engine's way just in time.

All around them cars honked and drivers shouted and cursed at them. Gunny ignored it all, concentrating on keeping the car in one lane and ahead of the bullets.

Sweat drenched his shirt and dripped into his eyes, but he stayed focused. The world narrowed to the path he was making through traffic.

Shards of glass rained down on them, and Junior let out another yelp. The back window had been shattered by a bullet. The tires screeched as Junior skidded the car to a stop at the mouth of an alleyway.

"Come on," Gunny said, flinging open his door. He practically fell onto the pavement.

He glanced back and saw the boy was too terrified to move. Gunny reached back into the car and dragged Junior out by his jacket.

"On your feet now!" Gunny ordered.

The steel in Gunny's voice must have jump-started Junior's brain. The boy's feet hit the sidewalk, and together they tore into the alley.

Dead end.

"This way," Junior said. Gunny watched the boy jump up to grab the steel rungs of the ladder on the fire escape, pulling the ladder down toward the ground. He clambered up, then turned and reached out his hand to Gunny.

"I can do it," Gunny snarled. He jumped up and gripped the cold metal. With a little huff, he hoisted himself the rest of the way up onto the fire escape. Then he followed Junior up to the roof.

In the street below, Gunny heard the unmistakable sound of bullets. "Down!" Gunny hissed. He pressed hard on Junior's shoulders, buckling the boy's knees. Gunny lay flat and peered over the edge of the roof; Junior did the same.

A nondescript black car sped by, and a volley of shots hit the car Junior had just been driving. *Whoosh!* The engine caught fire.

Gunny watched the flames, catching his breath. There were no more shots.

Junior rolled over and lay on his back, his body shuddering as he tried to calm his breathing. "Why would anyone want to kill me?" he asked in a hoarse whisper.

Gunny looked at the frightened boy. "You tell me."

Junior raised his eyes to Gunny's face. "I—I don't know."

Gunny frowned. Was Junior a target for some reason? Gunny shook off the thought as soon as he had it. It just didn't make enough sense. "Who knew you were driving Ambrose's car?" he asked.

Slowly Junior sat up. "Just Ambrose. And maybe some of the construction crew. We were at his site, and there was some problem. Ambrose couldn't get away, so he asked me to pick up the envelopes."

"The envelopes," Gunny said, putting it together. "Do you know what's inside them?"

Junior shrugged. "I never looked."

"Well, I think those people shooting at us resent giving Ambrose those little envelopes. You should stay away from him."

Junior quickly switched from bewildered and frightened to belligerent and defiant. "You sound just like my father."

Gunny flinched as he remembered the news he still had to deliver.

"Let's get out of here," Gunny said, offering Junior a hand up. "We need to go see your mother."

Junior crossed his arms over his chest and planted his feet. "That's right. You said something happened. And I'm not moving from this spot until you tell me what."

Gunny studied the boy. This was big. This wasn't a scolding about joyriding or staying out too late.

"Come on," Gunny said. "We have to go."

"I'm not going anywhere with you, old man, until you tell me why."

Junior's dark brown eyes never left Gunny's face. It was a stare-down, and Gunny realized he was going to blink first.

"It—it's your father."

Junior scowled. "He told you to come and get me, is that it? Well you tell him—"

"No," Gunny interrupted. "Someone shot him. He's dead."

Gunny watched Junior's face transform as the boy slowly comprehended the significance of what Gunny had just told him. His eyes widened and suddenly flicked to the ground. Junior swallowed a number of times, as if there were something trapped in his throat. His head shook, as if his brain were fighting off the knowledge that his father had been killed.

Gunny was at a loss for words. He had known Junior and his family all of the boy's life, but he had never been part of it. How do you comfort someone who is practically a stranger? And what did boys need to hear in moments like this anyway?

Jed was wrong, Gunny thought. *I am not up to this task*.

"I—I'm sorry, Junior," Gunny said. "Truly."

Junior took a deep breath and looked up at Gunny again.

"My mom. Delia. Are they okay?" he asked.

"They weren't harmed," Gunny assured him.

"I need to see them," Junior said, jogging toward the fire escape.

As upset by the news as Junior obviously was, Gunny noticed the boy's first thoughts were of the rest of his family. Gunny hadn't expected that.

Gunny and Junior walked through the door of the Wright apartment, just two floors below Jed's. Cousin Mary sat beside Delia, and three women Gunny recognized from the neighborhood were pouring coffee and setting out sandwiches.

A short, stout police officer stood by Mrs. Wright, scribbling notes in a notepad. "Tell me," the officer was saying, "can you think of anyone who might want to harm your husband?"

"No, no one." Mrs. Wright looked composed, but her dark skin was ashen, and she spoke faintly, as if she were far away. "Everyone loved Jeffrey."

Her eyes wandered the room, looking for confirmation. "Junior!"

Junior rushed over to his mother and they embraced. "Your father—he—"

"I know, Mama, I know," Junior told her.

"Thank you for bringing him home," Mrs. Wright said to Gunny over Jed's shoulder.

Junior released his mother and turned to the officer. "Do you have any suspects?" he asked, sounding very adult.

"Jed Sweeney was found with the gun," the policeman said. "He's in custody."

Junior's face went nearly purple with rage. "I'll kill him!"

"Now, son, calm down," the officer said mildly.

"I *knew* Jumpin' Jed would never let Daddy leave the band!" Junior shouted.

Uh-oh, Gunny thought. Junior was providing just the kind of motive the police were looking for. It confirmed the theory they already had, and they could simply call the case closed.

"Your father hadn't decided yet," Mrs. Wright argued. "And even if he had, Jed Sweeney certainly wouldn't have shot him over it. Now hush."

Junior's jaw set, but he stopped talking. He crossed his arms and leaned against the wall, glaring.

"Mama——," Delia began.

"Officer, clubs have been broken up before by rival gangster owners," Gunny said, interrupting Delia, trying to get things back on track. "Shouldn't you be looking at them?"

The policeman narrowed his eyes at Gunny. "And you are? . . ."

"Vincent Van Dyke, but everyone calls me 'Gunny.'"

"So, Mr. Van Dyke, what's your interest here?"

"My interest is the truth. And I know Jed Sweeney is innocent."

"Oh, you know that, do you?" The policeman sneered.

"Well, without Halliday or any other eyewitness, there's only so much we can do."

"Marvin still hasn't turned up?" Gunny asked.

"Nope. But the gun we found on your pal had its entire round shot. Not all the bullets were in Mr. Wright. They could be in Mr. Halliday."

"Or Marvin could be in hiding," Gunny suggested. The last thing Jed needed was to be suspected of killing Marvin, too. "He could be afraid to come forward."

Delia put down her sandwich. "Mama—"

"Not now, honey," Mrs. Wright said. "The grown-ups need to talk."

Delia rolled her eyes and left the room.

"We'll let you know if we find out anything," the officer said. He flipped his notepad shut. "Sorry for your loss, ma'am." He gave a little nod, then left the room.

Junior exploded. "How can you defend Jed Sweeney?" he shouted at Gunny. "He did this, and if you're on his side, then you're not on ours."

He turned and stormed into the other room, pulling the door behind him so hard the pictures on the living-room wall rattled.

Mrs. Wright turned a worried face to Gunny. "I don't believe Jed had anything to do with this. He's a victim too. Sitting in that jail."

"I'm glad to hear you believe in his innocence," Gunny said. "He's going to need all the supporters he can get. I think we're going to have quite a time convincing the police."

Gunny rubbed his face wearily. Junior wasn't going to make it any easier.

Six

The next morning Gunny headed for the subway stop. He had just left the Wrights' apartment after Jeffrey's funeral. Now he was going to check in on Jed.

There wasn't any action at Ambrose Jackson's site this time. But Ambrose was there, having what looked like a heated discussion with a construction worker— probably the site foreman. As Gunny drew closer, the argument grew louder.

"Not until my men get paid," the foreman was saying. He crossed his burly arms over his barrel chest.

"Don't fret, my man," Ambrose said with a broad smile. "You'll get your money. You know I'm good for it."

"I know food doesn't appear on my table unless I pay cash for it," the foreman said. "The grocer doesn't accept promises. And neither do I."

So Ambrose is having money problems, Gunny noted.

Ambrose's eyes narrowed and a steely glint appeared in them. He was still smiling, but the hard set of his jaw made it clear to Gunny that Ambrose was fighting back a boiling anger.

"I'll have all the money you need very soon," Ambrose assured the construction worker, his voice now clipped, rather than the smooth, velvety tones he usually used. "I've got a sure thing about to come in. It's going to hit, I know it."

The foreman looked skeptical. "The only sure thing I know is cash in my hand. So when you've got that, that's when we'll start working again." He turned and walked away.

Ambrose glared after him. Gunny suspected Ambrose was a man used to getting his way.

Something about the conversation set Gunny thinking. "Sure thing," "going to hit"—Gunny had heard gamblers use those phrases. Gunny had learned from hard experience that gambling and gunplay too often went hand in hand. If Ambrose sent Junior to pick up money from gamblers, that could explain why the car Junior was driving had been shot up.

"You there," Gunny called after Ambrose.

Ambrose turned to face Gunny. A wary smile slowly appeared. "You're Jumpin' Jed's pal," he said with a slow nod.

"I'm also a friend of the Wright family," Gunny said. "So I don't like it if any of them are put into a dangerous situation."

Ambrose's smile broadened. "Of course not. I feel the same way."

"Those envelopes you sent Junior to collect. Were they to pay off gambling debts?" Gunny asked.

"Is this guy bothering you, Mr. Jackson?"

Gunny startled. He hadn't heard the man who had just materialized behind him. The man strolled past Gunny and stood next to Ambrose.

"All good here," Ambrose said. "Though this gentleman should keep his nose out of other people's business."

Another man stepped up beside Ambrose. Where did they come from? Gunny realized they must have been hovering in the background and only drew attention to themselves when they thought Ambrose was in danger. Bodyguards—invisible until called into action. The bulges under their jackets were quite visible to Gunny now, though.

"I sincerely hope Junior and his family are faring well during this difficult time." Ambrose gave Gunny what looked like a sincere smile. Well, his lips were smiling but his eyes had a hard look to them. Then he gave his men a signal, and they all strolled away.

Gunny watched them as they turned the corner. He had a feeling if he was going to try to keep Junior safe, getting him away from Ambrose might be a good place to start.

Gunny perched on the edge of the rickety cot in Jed Sweeney's jail cell.

"The whole neighborhood turned out for the funeral this morning," he told Jed. "I think that made Mrs. Wright proud."

"How are Delia and Junior holding up?"

"Hard to say. They were very dignified at the funeral. Even Junior kept himself in check."

"Good."

"How does Ambrose Jackson figure with the Wrights?" Gunny asked. "Were he and Jeffrey close?"

"What does your gut tell you?" Jed asked.

"My gut usually just tells me it's time for lunch," Gunny joked.

"You should pay attention to your instincts," Jed said. "You can trust them. Listen to that inner voice and tell me what *you* think of Ambrose."

Jed had always been a bit eccentric but had never steered him wrong, so Gunny decided to try it. He shut his eyes and pictured Ambrose. He opened his eyes again. "Ambrose is bad news." He snorted a laugh. "But I don't think that's a particularly surprising conclusion to come to."

"Do you think he could be harmful to the Wrights?" Jed pressed.

"I don't think he has that boy's best interests in mind. But I don't know what kind of danger he could pose."

Jed nodded. "I've felt the same way about Ambrose since he started spending so much time in the neighborhood. Nothing I could put my finger on. There's just something . . ."

"Oily? Snakelike?"

Jed smiled. "Exactly."

"Is there a link between Marvin Halliday, Jeffrey Wright, and Ambrose Jackson?" Gunny asked.

"I did see the three of them together at times," Jed said. "And I know Jeffrey didn't want Junior doing errands for Ambrose."

Gunny shrugged. "That could be because the errands took Junior to bad neighborhoods or encouraged him to break laws."

"Don't let on to Mrs. Wright," Jed said, "but I often loaned Jeffrey money, and so did other members of the band. Money we never saw again. He always promised he'd have it any day now but . . ."

Gunny's eyebrows raised. "Do you know what Jeffrey needed the money for?"

Jed shook his head. "I always assumed it was for the kids. I never had any of my own, but I do know raising a family is expensive."

"Could he have been gambling?" Gunny asked.

Jed shrugged. "Could be. Do you think that's why Marvin's club was smashed up, and Jeffrey killed? Over gambling debts?"

"I'm beginning to think that's exactly why—and I think Ambrose had something to do with it."

Jed's dark eyes widened. "Then it's even more important you keep an eye on Junior. If he's spending time with Ambrose . . ."

"I know," Gunny said. "Junior could be heading for deep trouble."

The next evening the party to raise bail money for Jed was in full swing at the Wrights' apartment when Gunny arrived. He was surprised when Mrs. Wright suggested she host it, until she explained that she just wanted to keep busy. "Besides," she added, "I want everyone to know I don't hold Jed responsible. Even Junior sees that now."

Gunny paid his dollar at the door and scanned the

room. Jed would be proud to see how many people not only believed he was innocent but were willing to share their hard-earned dollars to try to help him. A buffet table was filled with potluck dishes and music blared from the radio. Several couples were dancing to the new hot swing.

Delia gave Gunny a shy wave. "Where's your brother?" he asked when he joined her.

Delia frowned. "He won't come out of his room," she said.

"I'll go have a chat with him," Gunny said.

He lightly rapped on the door, but didn't wait for a response; he just turned the knob. He had a feeling Junior wouldn't have let him in if given an option.

The room was dark, but Gunny could make out Junior lying on his bed. The boy was on his stomach, gazing through the window.

"Leave me alone," Junior said.

"Just came in to see how you are."

"Fine."

"Now, son, don't go telling lies. I wouldn't be fine if I had just lost my father."

"What do you want me to do?" Junior demanded, not turning his head. "Bust out crying?"

Gunny grimaced. He was saying all the wrong things. Why did Jed keep insisting that he do this?

He heard a commotion of some sort on the other side of the door, but concentrated on Junior. "Well, if you feel like crying—"

"I don't!" Junior flipped over onto his back. "I feel like being left alone."

"Your Mama says—"

Three quick raps on the door interrupted Gunny. Three raps in slower succession, then three fast ones again got Junior to swing his feet to the floor. He stared at the door.

"Junior?" Gunny asked.

"Something's wrong," Junior said. "That's our code. Delia and me."

The raps came again, with more urgency this time.

"SOS," Gunny said, recognizing the sequence from his army training.

Junior crossed the room in three long steps and opened the door.

Delia grabbed his hand. "Mama's upset. Come quick."

Gunny followed the children into the main room. Now he understood the commotion. Chubby Malloy had arrived.

"You have a lot of nerve showing up here!" a voice in the crowd shouted.

"We're trying to raise money for a man who is in jail instead of you!" someone else shouted.

Chubby looked grim, but the thugs with him looked a lot grimmer.

Mrs. Wright glared at the men. "I've already asked you to leave. And I don't want to ask you again."

Junior pushed his way quickly through the group. "You heard my mother. You get out of here. Now!"

To Gunny's complete shock, Junior spit in the huge man's face.

Instantly the thugs had guns trained on Junior.

Without thinking for even a split second, Gunny stepped in between Junior and the weapons. Just in time to hear the click of the triggers being cocked.

SEVEN

The boy just lost his father," Gunny said softly, forcing himself to sound calm, even though he could feel his heart thudding against his ribs.

How did he keep winding up with guns pointing straight at him?

The room was silent as Gunny and Chubby stared at each other.

"Grief does crazy things to people," Gunny said.

Now Chubby's eyes narrowed and Gunny could tell the club owner was weighing his options. Then he held up one hand to signal his men not to move and pulled a handkerchief from his pocket with the other. Slowly he wiped his face.

"He gets a pass," Chubby said, his voice low and serious. "Once."

"Understood," Gunny said.

The gangsters put away their guns, and Gunny's shoulders dropped back down to where they belonged, instead of hunched up by his ears.

Chubby threw up his thick arms in exasperation. "What I don't understand," he demanded loudly, "is why everyone seems to think I had anything to do with this mess." He looked around the room. Gunny noted that no one would meet Chubby's gaze.

"I don't have to worry about Marvin Halliday and his sorry club. No one can compete with my Paradise," Chubby huffed. "Why should I care if some drum player wants to set out on his own?" He seemed genuinely perplexed. Hurt, even.

There were shuffling feet, averted eyes, and a few murmurs around the room, but no one spoke.

Chubby's hurt look was replaced by flashing anger. "I don't have to take this." He yanked a fistful of dollar bills out of the "bail bowl." "And I'm not giving a dime to Jed's defense. In fact," Chubby continued, lumbering back and forth in front of the door, "because of this insult, I'm going to *fire* Jumpin' Jed's JiveMasters!"

Someone in the room gasped, but no one dared to say anything. Gunny knew everyone was afraid of making the situation worse.

"Yeah, yeah." Chubby nodded, as if he were warming to the notion. "I think I'll go ahead with that championship boxing idea I had." He rubbed his palms together and tipped his head toward his goons. "Don't need a band for that, do you?"

"No, boss," a thug said. "No band. Just a loud bell!"

Chubby let out a hooting laugh and clapped a beefy hand on the goon's broad shoulder. "You got that right!"

Chubby snapped his fingers, and he and his two bodyguards spun on their heels in unison, and the three men walked out. The room instantly felt bigger.

The moment they left, the room burst into loud chatter. Gunny stared at the door that had just shut behind Chubby. Chubby's genuine bewilderment and hurt had made a real impact. Gunny felt in his gut that Chubby wasn't behind the hit. But if everyone, including the police, thought the culprit was either Chubby or Jumpin' Jed, how would Gunny convince anyone to investigate somebody else?

By getting the evidence himself.

One day after the bail party, Gunny walked down the basement corridor of the Manhattan Tower Hotel toward his room. After seeing Jed in jail, Gunny had so much on his mind he felt as if his head would explode. He passed the hotel laundry, the vault, and the baggage room, and arrived at the door to his apartment. He was looking forward to stretching out on his bed, if only for a catnap.

He stopped.

The door was slightly ajar. He rarely locked his door, but he certainly hadn't left it open, that much he knew.

He held his breath and listened at the door.

He heard a tiny scraping sound, as if someone had pushed a chair away from a table.

No doubt about it. Someone was inside.

EiGHt

Treading as softly as he could, and keeping his eyes on the door, Gunny backed away. He kept his eyes on the door just in case the intruder stepped out.

He ran his hand along the wall so that he'd know when he'd arrived at the laundry room. He needed a weapon, and the closest he'd find to one would be in here.

The steamy air was filled with the scent of bleach and crisp smell of linen in the presses. He moved quickly— he didn't want the intruder to slip away before he could discover who was there, and why.

His eyes landed on the long dowels used to open the windows to allow steam to escape. At the basement level the windows were small and hard to reach; they could only be opened from the very top. He grabbed a dowel and tiptoed quickly back to his apartment. The door was still ajar.

Holding the dowel in front of him as if it were a javelin, he charged his apartment. The door flew open and slammed hard against the wall. There was a high-pitched, terrified shriek and then a crash. A chair toppled over as a small figure ducked under the table.

Gunny quickly switched his grip so he could swing the pole at the intruder's head. His heart thudded as adrenaline pumped through him.

"It's me! Don't hurt me!"

Gunny blinked. Still gripping the dowel, he bent down and peered under the table.

Two huge brown eyes in a round, dark face peered back.

"Delia, what are you doing here?" Gunny demanded. He couldn't believe he'd been frightened by an eleven-year-old girl. He crossed to the window and balanced the dowel in the corner. "Does your mother know where you are?" he asked.

Delia looked away, which answered Gunny's question.

"Delia," Gunny said with a scolding tone. Before he could say anything further, the phone jangled. He picked it up. "Yes?"

"Gunny!"

Mrs. Wright's distraught voice came though loud and clear over the phone.

"Don't worry, Martha," Gunny said, knowing exactly why she sounded so upset. "Delia is here with me."

"I was so worried," Mrs. Wright said. "She simply disappeared. With Junior I wouldn't have been so surprised, but Delia has never given me any cause for worry."

Gunny kept his eye on the girl. She was walking around his room, gazing at the picture on his wall.

"Well, with all that's been happening," Gunny said softly, not wanting Delia to overhear them discussing her, "the girl probably just needed to get away for a bit."

"I suppose. She's going to get quite the talking-to though. Going all the way to your place on her own. And scaring me half to death."

Delia had also scared *Gunny* half to death, but he wasn't going to admit that!

"I'll bring her home myself," Gunny promised Mrs. Wright, then hung up.

Delia was studying him, an impatient look on her face.

"Something bothering you, little missy?" Gunny asked.

"I'm here because I think I know where Marvin Halliday might be," she said. "Don't you need him as a witness—to help Jumpin' Jed?"

Gunny gaped at Delia. This little girl could accomplish what the police and the adults in her neighborhood couldn't? Discover the whereabouts of the prime witness?

"You're going to catch flies with your mouth hanging open like that," Delia snapped. "Don't act so surprised. I know things."

"I guess you do at that," Gunny said. "Why do you think you can help us find Mr. Halliday?"

Delia shrugged. "Everyone thinks I'm just a little kid. And a Goody Two-shoes. They hardly notice me. So they talk in front of me. Daddy often took me with him to the club or on errands when Mama was working. I heard things."

Now Gunny was curious. What did the child think she knew? "Go on. Where do you think Marvin Halliday is?"

Delia smiled. She obviously enjoyed having someone take her seriously.

"Daddy and Mr. Halliday both liked the ponies," Delia said. "I thought if Mr. Halliday was upset about his club being ruined, maybe he'd go to where the ponies are. I went to the stables near Central Park, but no one I asked knew him. I thought maybe you would know some other place where you can be with ponies."

Interesting. Ambrose talked about having a "sure thing" coming in, and now it seemed that both Marvin and Jeffrey "liked the ponies." This was adding up to a shared taste for gambling. And if both Marvin and Jeffrey owed money because of gambling—quite possibly to Ambrose—that could explain the motive right there. Ambrose was very quick to point the finger at Chubby.

"You are an enterprising young lady," Gunny said.

Delia's face lit up at the compliment.

"Let me ask you something," Gunny continued, amazed that he was using an eleven-year-old girl as a sounding board. "The police believe Jed might be guilty because your father was quitting the band. What do *you* think?"

"Daddy wasn't going to do that," Delia said firmly. "I asked him and he said he liked it over at Chubby Malloy's. I guess he didn't get a chance to tell Mama—" Her voice broke off and Gunny was afraid she might cry. "So *I* told her. And Junior. Now even Junior knows it wasn't Jed or Chubby."

"Junior believed you?" Gunny asked.

Delia shrugged. "Junior is still real mad. He just doesn't know who to be mad at. So I think that makes him even madder."

She gazed down at the floor. She swallowed hard and then her eyes widened. "Do you think Mr. Halliday was so mad about Daddy staying with Jed at Chubby's that *he* killed Daddy?"

Smart kid, Gunny thought. *She's found an angle that hadn't occurred to any of us.* "I don't think so. That wouldn't explain why Mr. Halliday's club got all smashed up."

Delia looked relieved. "That's good. Daddy liked Mr. Halliday. It would be terrible if his friend was the one who shot him."

"What about Ambrose Jackson?" Gunny asked. "Were he and your father friends?"

Delia pursed her lips in thought. She shook her head. "They acted like it, but I could tell Daddy really didn't like Mr. Jackson. He was nervous around him." She scowled. "I don't like him either. He talks sweet, but it's all fake."

"Thank you, Delia. You have been very helpful." Kids see things adults don't, Gunny realized. Most of the neighborhood seemed to consider Ambrose a great guy. The more he thought about it, the more he believed Ambrose was the guilty party.

Now he just had to prove it.

"Running all over town when I should be trying to raise money for Jed," Gunny muttered. "Or finding evidence to nail Ambrose." He pulled the collar of his coat higher. The rain was not improving his mood.

He had just come back from seeing Jed in jail. Both agreed that the police wouldn't simply accept Delia's information—that her father had no intention of leaving Jed's band—to clear Jed, even though it proved he had no motive. So Gunny was even more determined to find the proof linking Ambrose to the murder. He had a feeling the link would involve gambling.

What surprised Gunny was that Jed still seemed more concerned about Gunny watching over Junior than he was in his own case. So here he was, keeping tabs on the boy.

The soaking rain didn't wash away the broken bottles or garbage littering the uneven streets. No wonder Jeffrey and Junior argued—if Gunny were Junior's father, he wouldn't want Junior spending his time down here either.

Odd. In the dark neighborhood two windows glowed just below ground level. Faint sounds of shouting and laughter emanated from them. Something was going on in that warehouse basement.

Gunny carefully made his way down the slick metal steps and peered in the grimy windows. "My, my, my," he breathed.

He wasn't sure what he had expected to see, but it wasn't a boxing ring and a professional-looking match under way!

He snapped his fingers. Boxing. Junior wanted to learn to be a boxer and his father objected.

"Might as well dry off," Gunny told himself.

The smell of sweat, blood, and cigar smoke assaulted Gunny as soon as he opened the door. He shook the rain off as he stepped inside.

"Don't let the weather in!" a gruff man in shirtsleeves and a colorful vest snarled.

Gunny pulled the door shut behind him and turned to face the ring. Shouts and catcalls bounced off the low ceilings, and the room was dark. All the lights seemed to be aimed at the ring.

He paid his admission and moved away from the door. A fight was already in progress. A small wiry fighter, his dark skin coated with sweat, was ducking and swaying. A thicker, more powerful man was jabbing. The smaller man dodged and feinted.

"Look at that speed," the man in the vest said with admiration. "He's like a ballet dancer."

Gunny nodded. The smaller fighter had a lithe, catlike way of moving that made the bigger man look stodgy.

"But does he have power?" Gunny asked. "Heart?"

The man in the vest nodded. "This is his third fight tonight. I'm betting he'll win this one too."

"He's doesn't even look tired!" Gunny said, amazed.

The man in the vest shoved a fat, stinky cigar into his mouth. "He's young."

Gunny's eyes adjusted to the low light, and he recognized a few faces. Interesting. Both Chubby Malloy and Ambrose Jackson were focused intently on the ring.

The fighters were circling now, and Gunny's mouth dropped open. The smaller fighter was Junior!

Now he could make out what the crowd down near the ring was shouting: "Kid Wright! Kid Wright!"

If Junior has a nickname, he must come here a lot,

Gunny realized. No one seemed to be rooting for the bigger guy. Junior was a definite favorite.

Gunny's eyes went back to the ring. *No wonder*, he thought. The kid was good! In a flurry of moves, an uppercut, a twist, and a body blow, the larger fighter was suddenly down on the mat. A roar went up, the referee made the count, the bell rang and Junior had won again.

"Kid Wright doesn't seem able to lose," the man in the vest said, smiling. "The payouts are smaller because he's such a sure thing. It's nice to know there are things in life a man can count on."

Three men helped drag the loser out of the ring, while Junior beamed and waved his gloved hands. Then he ducked under the ropes and out of the ring. He stood nearby, gulping down water.

"Up next!" an announcer declared, "Kid Wright and Action Anderson."

Gunny sensed an immediate change in the crowd. He could feel the tension rise and there were whispers all around. Gunny wondered who this Action Anderson was.

A hulking giant lumbered into the ring. On the other side of the ropes, Junior suddenly went back to looking like a boy again. A small one.

"That guy will kill Junior!" Gunny exclaimed.

He pushed his way down to the ring. *This is crazy*, he thought. Why would anyone want such a mismatched competition?

Someone who wanted Junior to lose. *If Junior is the favorite, and someone bets on his opponent, the payout would be huge if Junior loses.*

"Junior!" Gunny clamped a hand on Junior's shoulder.

"What are you doing here?" Junior asked. He shrugged off Gunny's hand. "You're going to try to stop me, aren't you." He glared at Gunny. "Just like my dad."

"You bet I am," Gunny said. "You can't go into the ring with that gorilla."

"You don't think I'm any good."

"That's just it—you *are* good. You could probably be great, but you have to live long enough to train," Gunny said. "That guy will do you major damage—maybe permanently."

Suddenly Chubby Malloy appeared on Junior's other side. "Listen to him, Kid. Don't go out losing, go out victorious!"

Gunny tensed. The last time Chubby and Junior met, Junior spit in the large man's face. Yet Chubby stood here giving Junior good advice. Clearly, Chubby had forgotten about that incident. Junior was another story. According to Delia, Junior now agreed that neither Jed nor Chubby killed his father. But that was according to an eleven-year-old girl. . . .

Junior's jaw clenched. Was he still blaming Chubby? Gunny wondered. Would he do something foolish—and potentially dangerous?

"Chubby's right," Gunny advised. "He doesn't want you hurt. And you will be if you go into that ring."

Junior looked at Chubby, who nodded. Junior's shoulders slumped.

"But everyone will think I'm chicken!" Junior protested.

"No, they'll think you're smart."

"But Ambrose says—"

"Forget about Ambrose!" Gunny snapped. "That man is only trouble. He doesn't have your best interests in mind. Believe me."

Junior stared at Gunny. Gunny hadn't meant to speak quite so forcefully.

Junior's eyes widened and his brow furrowed. "Do you think that Ambrose had something to do with my father—"

Before Junior could finish the sentence, a towering man in a cheap, shiny suit stepped up to them. "In the ring," a man ordered Junior. "Now."

"Who are you?" Gunny asked.

"I'm the owner," the man replied. "And Junior here was paid for four bouts. Unless, of course, he got knocked out. And clearly, Kid Wright is still standing."

"This is a ridiculous pairing," Chubby told the owner. "And everyone here knows it." He faced Junior. "I want you to stay in one piece, Kid. I'd like you to be a local contender at my club. I'm putting in regular bouts."

Junior's eyes widened in amazement. "Really?"

"But if you get your brains rattled or your eyes popped out in a fight with that giant over there," Gunny said, "you're not ever going to get that shot."

"The man speaks true," Chubby said.

Junior looked from Gunny to Chubby. "I guess you're right," he said finally.

"Good!" Chubby grinned. "Let's go outside to talk. It's too hard to hear in here." Chubby led Junior toward the door.

What a turn of events, Gunny thought as he followed them. He and Chubby working *together* to help Junior! And Junior was actually letting them! He finally had some good news to report to Jed.

A huge paw landed on Gunny's shoulder. The owner.

Do they grow them extrabig for this club? Gunny wondered. Gunny was a big man himself, but the owner towered over him.

"A fight is starting in thirty seconds," the owner said.

"Sorry, can't stay." Gunny squirmed to get out of the man's grip. It didn't work.

"If Junior isn't back in the ring, someone had better take his place."

"Fine by me," Gunny said. "Now I really do need to catch up with my—"

"These people paid money to see four fights," the owner said, his eyes narrowing. "Since you're the one who talked Junior out of fighting, I guess you're the one who has to tell them there won't be a fight. And you can refund all that money."

The crowd was growing impatient. Boos and catcalls and angry shouts filled the air.

Gunny took in a deep breath and let it out again in a long, slow exhale. "I guess Action Anderson will be facing Gunny Van Dyke tonight," Gunny said grimly.

NINE

There seemed to be nearly as much laughter as cheering when Gunny stepped into the ring. The shorts the owner found for him to wear were ratty, and the sleeves on the robe were miles too short. The gloves didn't fit much better.

There was a flurry of activity throughout the club when the patrons realized this wasn't some joke. Changing their bets, Gunny figured. The only person who sat still in his seat, a big grin on his face, was Ambrose. He must have bet on Action in the first place.

"Grandpa!" Action Anderson jeered. "This is going to be easy!"

"I'm not your grandpa," Gunny snapped.

The referee had them touch gloves. "Have a good clean fight," he said.

Gunny suspected that "good" and "clean" weren't in Action's vocabulary.

Clang! Action's fist connected with Gunny's cheekbone before the final reverberation of the starting bell had sounded. Gunny's head whipped back, but his hands instinctively blocked Action's next move.

Gunny sprang backward. He had to get a sense of Action's style. Action was younger, more experienced, outweighed him, and had serious power behind each blow: Gunny needed to fight smart, not hard.

They circled once around, Action tossing out little jabs and laughing, as if it were all a big game. Gunny stayed focused, moving, studying, learning. *Action leans to the right*, Gunny noted as he blocked an uppercut.

A shout from the crowd made Action's eyes flick to the ropes. He grinned, then he came in with another hook. It missed the mark.

That failed punch gave Gunny crucial information: Action wasn't paying complete attention. And he lurched off balance if he had to reach out to connect with Gunny.

Good, good, Gunny told himself, moving in an ever-widening circle. *That's it, keep laughing, Action. I've got some surprises for you.*

Everything beyond Action fell away for Gunny. The room became a black backdrop, the shouts and calls from the crowd a dull, oceanlike roar. All that mattered was sensing Action's next move.

Gunny had done some boxing in the army, and his muscles began to remember the training from long ago. His body recalled the twists, the ducks, the feints. His hands picked up speed, letting him land now more than he missed.

Action is a brawler, Gunny noted. *A slugger who relies on a power punch, not footwork or finesse.* Action's follow-ups were slow—he didn't work combinations. And, more important, he followed a predictable pattern.

If I can stay out of reach, avoid Action's one good punch, I might have a shot. Gunny couldn't match Action's power, but he had speed that the big lug didn't have.

"Don't want to get in and dance, Grandpa?" Action taunted. "You're staying awfully far away."

"Don't like your breath," Gunny snapped. But Action's comment made him think. Action wasn't paying complete attention because he underestimated Gunny. Let him.

Gunny began to slow down a bit, breathing heavily, as if he were already getting worn out. The more he faked it, the more Action smirked—and the sloppier Action became.

Crack! Blood spurted from Action's nose. Surprise crossed Action's ugly broad face, swiftly replaced by anger.

Action's right hook shot out toward Gunny's ribs, and Gunny stepped backward rather than block. Frustrated, Action's left immediately followed—not a good move for Action—taking him slightly off balance. That little wobble gave Gunny his opening. He rushed in with two sharp blows to Action's midsection, then an uppercut that knocked Action's head up and back. He stumbled into the ropes. Gunny pounced, pummeling the huge fighter, sensing the fight leaving his opponent. At last Action sank to the floor of the ring.

"Eight . . . nine . . . ten!" The referee blew his whistle after Action failed to get up on his own. The bell clanged, and the crowd roared. The referee grabbed Gunny's wrist and held his arm aloft to take in the cheers.

"I got beat by a grandpa," Action mumbled. "An old man."

"I may look old to you, sonny," Gunny said, "but I'm not out."

Dazed, Gunny made his way out of the ring. People clapped him on the back, congratulating him. But Gunny just wanted to get dressed and out of there.

The cold night air refreshed him. The rain had left the street smelling a bit better. Gunny chanced a deep breath. His ribs were sore, his face hurt, but he didn't think anything was broken.

"Where's Chubby?" Gunny asked Junior, who stood leaning against the building.

Junior straightened up quickly. "What happened to your face?" Junior asked. "You're bleeding!"

Gunny's reached up and tentatively touched his cheek. He pulled his hand away and saw the blood. He hadn't been aware of it in the ring.

The door flew open and Ambrose Jackson and his entourage piled out of the club. They were all in high spirits.

"Great showing!" Ambrose told Gunny. "When you got in the ring with Action, I thought you'd bought it for sure!" He and his group climbed into a waiting car. "Gotta hand it to you—you got heart, baby!" Ambrose called out the window. "Even if you did cost me a bundle of cash!" The car sped away.

Junior gaped at Gunny. "*You* did the fight?"

Gunny shrugged it off. "I took your spot. But you shouldn't have been there in the first place. This is a dangerous neighborhood and those fights aren't regulated. It's just too risky."

"It's the only place I can make money boxing," Junior

said. "I need to—I have to help out. Now that . . ." His voice trailed off.

"Not this way, Junior," Gunny said gently. "Your father would be proud that you want to take over as the man in the family. But he wouldn't want you to get hurt for it."

"But he just wouldn't listen!" Junior exploded. "Not about Ambrose. Not about boxing." Pain contorted his features, and he looked back down at his feet.

"Your dad was right about Ambrose," Gunny said. "You have to stay away from that man."

Junior studied Gunny's face. "You think it was Ambrose who killed my father?"

Gunny looked down at the ground. He worried what Junior would do if he confirmed Junior's suspicion.

"You do, don't you!" Junior exploded. "I'll kill him!"

Exactly what Gunny did *not* want to hear. Gunny grabbed Junior's arms and held him firmly in place. "You will do no such thing," he ordered. "You try anything with Ambrose and it's *your* life that's over, not his."

"But he—"

"He will come at you with guns blazing," Gunny said. "Let the adults handle it."

"I'm not a little kid!" Junior shouted. "I need to—"

"You need to stay safe," Gunny cut him off. "For your mother. For Delia."

Now it was Junior who stared down at the ground. Gunny hoped his words had sunk in. If Junior went after Ambrose, Gunny would have failed to keep his promise to Jed.

"In that ring," Gunny said, "Junior, you were really good. I bet your dad would have come around to boxing. In time."

Junior looked up with a grateful, hopeful expression. "You think?"

"I *know*."

Junior's huge, relieved smile made Gunny think for the first time that maybe, just maybe, Jed wasn't crazy to have asked him to watch out for Junior.

TEN

The previous day's rain had left the racetrack muddy. The early morning sun hadn't had a chance to do its work, and the horses were kicking up mud as they went through their paces.

This was the closest racetrack—the one Marvin and Jeffrey would most likely have attended if they had a thing for the ponies. The question was, would Gunny also find something to link them both to Ambrose? And, more important, would he find Marvin Halliday alive and kicking?

It was still early and most of the folks there now were with the race or die-hard gamblers trying to scout the winners by watching the warm-ups. If Marvin or Jeffrey were regulars, these were the people who would know it.

My, my, my. Delia was right. A very agitated Marvin Halliday was right at trackside. Other spectators were scattered along the track, but they seemed to have an unspoken agreement to keep out of one another's way.

Gunny tromped down to the track. "Where have

you been?" he demanded, startling Marvin. "Everyone's looking for you—me, the cops, everyone!"

A horrified expression crossed Marvin's face. "You can't tell anyone you found me!"

Gunny was taken aback. That was not the response he had expected. "You know that Jed has been arrested, right? The cops are even wondering if you're dead."

Marvin laughed hollowly. "Faking my own death could be a solution . . ."

"You've got to come with me now. Go to the cops."

Marvin shook his head. "Not a chance."

"But Jed—"

Marvin cut him off. "Jed will get off—he's innocent."

"There's no guarantee of that," Gunny argued. "There's a lot of evidence against him." Then the significance of Marvin's words hit him. "You know for a fact that Jed's innocent, because you saw who did it!"

Marvin noticed someone over Gunny's shoulder and went pale. "I've got to get out of here—now!"

"NO! You're coming with me!" Gunny shouted. He grabbed Marvin's arms. With a huge surge of energy, Marvin let out a loud bellow and shoved Gunny hard. Gunny stumbled and Marvin slipped away.

He righted himself, and now the streams of fans pouring into the track blocked his path. He gazed up into the stands. They were filling up fast. He didn't see Marvin anywhere.

But he did see Mr. Ambrose Jackson. Gunny was more certain than ever that Ambrose was the guy Marvin was hiding from—*and* Jeffrey Wright's killer.

"That mud is going to change things," said a short

slim man taking a spot next to Gunny near the guardrail. He stared down at the racing form in his hands. "And I had my winners all picked."

"Play the ponies a lot?" Gunny asked.

"Every chance I get." The man grinned. "You?"

"First time for me."

The man's smile broadened. "Oh, then let me tell you all about it! You need a system. And you gotta know all about the jockeys, and which horses like the mud and which need hard turf—"

The blare of the announcements drowned out the lecture by the friendly man.

The man leaned into Gunny. "I've got money on Red Robin. He's the favorite to win, so I won't get a big return. But I do like a sure thing!"

The horses were at the gate. The gun let out a *crack!* and they were off!

The blaring loudspeakers kept up a fast-paced, nonstop patter of unfamiliar names, though Gunny could pick out Red Robin in the buzzing announcements.

"Come on, come on, come on," the friendly man chanted, becoming more and more tense. "What are you *doing*?"

Gunny could see that the lead horse was dropping back. Another horse surged steadily ahead, its legs a blur of motion and mud. How could it move so fast? Gunny wondered.

Within moments the new horse crossed the finish line.

"No!" The friendly man threw his hands up in the air. "Not possible!"

"In a surprise upset," the announcer's voice blared from the speakers, "Gladiator took the field and won the race!" The announcer sounded as stunned as the friendly man beside Gunny.

"He's not as good a horse?" Gunny asked.

"Nowhere near!" the friendly man said. "Gladiator was the long shot. You wouldn't even bet on that horse to place in the top three, much less win." He stared back down at the form again. "Gotta figure all the percentages differently now," he was muttering as Gunny walked away.

With the first race over, Gunny went back to searching for Marvin. There was a large crowd near the windows where the gamblers placed bets and collected winnings. Mostly he saw grim expressions.

He saw one smiling face though: Ambrose! He had just turned away from the teller's window with a big grin on his face. So Ambrose was the one lucky guy to bet on the winning horse?

Or, Gunny thought, *he has inside information.*

Which meant Gunny had to find himself an insider.

Horse trailers, grooms, horses, jockeys, and owners crowded the grounds in the busy stable area. It was easy to spot the differences: The owners were dressed in their Sunday best, the jockeys were little fellas in brightly colored silks, some of the grooms wore the same colors as the jockeys, while still others wore regular work clothes. There were also folks who seemed to work for the track who were the least gussied-up of all. Gunny figured with his bruised face, mud-spattered coat from standing ringside, and rumpled shirt, he'd have his best shot at pretending to be with the track.

He spotted a groom unloading a bale of hay from a trailer.

"Let me help you there, sonny," Gunny said.

"Thanks!" The groom smiled gratefully. He looked about eighteen. "I need to get this into King Rex's stall, but Mr. Sheffield wants me to walk King Rex around in front of some photographers."

"Owners!" Gunny snorted knowingly. "Can't seem to understand you can't be in two places at once."

The groom laughed as they lowered the bale to the ground. "Why don't I bring this to King Rex's stall," Gunny offered. "Your owner won't care who makes the delivery. If he's like most owners, he's far more interested in the bright lights."

"Really?" The groom looked up at Gunny with a grateful expression.

"Gotta do a check inside anyway," Gunny said.

"Thanks! I owe you!" The groom helped Gunny load the bale onto a dolly, explained which stall King Rex was in, and took off.

Gunny dragged the dolly inside, dropped off the hay at King Rex's empty stall, then went in search of the winning horse and his jockey.

"Gladiator, Gladiator," Gunny muttered, looking at the names posted on the stall doors. He moved deeper and deeper into the stable. There were fewer people in this area; with the races now under way, most of the horses had been brought outside for exercise.

But Gunny didn't want to talk to the jockey or groom of a horse that was about to race; he was after the people associated with the horse that had just won Ambrose big money.

He heard stomping and whinnying a few rows down.

Gunny hurried over and looked at the sign on the door. Gladiator. The long shot.

The horse was in the stall alone. It looked odd—agitated. Not that Gunny knew much about horses, but there was definitely something wrong with the animal.

"You're worried over nothing," a nearby voice said.

Ambrose, Gunny realized. *Heading this way.*

Gunny dragged a stack of hay away from the back wall and slipped behind it.

"What if we get caught?" another voice said.

Gunny peeked through a gap in the hay bales. Ambrose was with a jockey.

"Doping a horse is a serious offense," the jockey said.

"So we have to make sure no one finds out, don't we?" Ambrose said.

"What if they test the horse? Or Randall squeals?" the jockey asked, his voice rising in panic. "What if people find out that he threw the race?"

"What if? What if?" Ambrose repeated in a singsong imitation of the jockey. Then his voice grew cold. "Randall won't be talking. Neither will the horse. Or you!"

In a single swift blow, Ambrose knocked out the jockey and shoved him into the stall with the drugged horse.

"People really shouldn't smoke with all this straw and wood around," Ambrose said, pulling a cigarette and a box of matches from his pocket. "Filthy habit."

He dropped the lit cigarette and match into the dry straw. In moments there was a fast-growing blaze.

Ambrose shut the stall door and left, his cackle rising above the horse's terrified whinnying and the roar of the flames.

ELEVEN

Smoke made Gunny's eyes tear. He covered his nose and mouth with his arm and dragged the unconscious jockey into a corner. The horse was going crazy; Gunny didn't want the jockey crushed under its pounding hooves.

He yanked off his coat and grabbed a horse blanket and tossed them onto the nearest flames. He flung himself down and rolled back and forth, feeling the heat from the burning hay under him while desperately trying to avoid the terrified horse. Luckily, the horse was intent on trying to break down the stall door.

Flames licked up the wooden sides of the stall. Gunny leaped up and grabbed the blanket, but it fell apart in his hands. He tried to call for help, but the smoke made him cough and choke.

Foam and spittle dripped from Gladiator's mouth, and its eyes rolled in terror. The drugs Ambrose doped the horse with made its panic worse—but it also made it powerful. The wooden door began to splinter.

Could Gunny use the fire to help weaken the door? It

was a terrible risk—making the fire worse—but it might be the only way out.

He picked up a flaming bundle of hay and shoved it into the slats at the top of the stall. He leaped out of the way just in time to avoid being kicked in the head by Gladiator.

The wooden door caught fire. The horse surrounded on all sides by flames, let out a terrified shriek. It spun around, searching for a way out. It reared up.

"The door!" Gunny yelled at the horse as he flung himself away from Gladiator's landing hooves. "Kick the door!"

Gunny's shouts panicked the horse more, but as it bucked, its back hooves kicked out.

And the door fell off its hinges.

Gladiator let out a whinny. Gunny flattened into the corner as the horse twisted and thundered away.

Most of the hay was on fire. Gunny grabbed what was left of his coat and stomped out the fabric that was burning, then threw it over the jockey, patting him down. He lifted the unconscious jockey with a grunt. If the jockey had been the size of an ordinary man, Gunny would never have been able to stumble out of the smoke-filled space. But jockeys were small, and Gunny managed to get them both out of the stall.

Grooms and workers streamed into the stable with buckets of water. At some point an alarm must have sounded, but Gunny had been too intent on escape to hear it.

He brought the jockey outside into the fresh air, where someone could attend him. Gasping for breath, woozy, and coughing, Gunny stumbled to a nearby tree. He slid down the trunk to the ground and shut his eyes.

When he opened them again, he was confronted by the terrible sight of Gladiator, down on the ground. Not moving. Not breathing.

The drugs, Gunny thought. *That's what killed that poor animal.* But now everyone would assume it was smoke inhalation and panic. Ambrose got away with it. And the jockey would be much too terrified to say a word. Or to back up Gunny's accusation.

He still had no proof, but Gunny knew beyond a shadow of a doubt that Ambrose was up to his eyeballs in gambling and fixing events.

And he also knew just how far Ambrose was willing to go to get what he wanted.

TWELVE

Things were finally looking up. Chubby himself contributed to the bail fund and Gunny was able to spring Jed. Tonight Gunny and Jed were going to spend time together as if they didn't have a care in the world. And they were going to do it at Chubby's nightclub, watching Junior fight.

Every night that week, Gunny went to Chubby Malloy's Paradise to watch Junior fight. The kid was good, and had quickly become a favorite. Even better, the boy had steered clear of Ambrose.

At least until now! Gunny did a double take when he saw Junior enter accompanied by Ambrose. Ambrose had his arm slung casually over Junior's shoulder and was grinning his usual irritating smile, but Junior looked . . . Gunny couldn't actually read the boy's expression. Something was wrong, though. Could Junior have confronted Ambrose about shooting Jeffrey?

Not likely, Gunny decided. If such a showdown had taken place, Gunny didn't think Junior would still be around to fight this fight. And there'd be evidence of a much bigger problem than the obvious tension he saw between them.

The bell sounded and Junior shook off Ambrose's arm. He stepped into the ring. Gunny craned his neck, searching for Jed. He was missing the first fight!

No matter. *He'll be here when he gets here*, Gunny decided, and concentrated on Junior in the ring.

Junior was well matched with another featherweight. Gunny had seen the two fight before. Each had their strengths. Only, tonight Junior's strengths were not in evidence. He seemed . . . distracted.

Gunny had only ever seen Junior fight with passion and intense focus. The kid was still landing his punches, still avoiding the hits, but he was off. Like his heart wasn't in it.

Maybe he's getting tired of the game, Gunny observed. But Gunny wouldn't have expected that from Junior. He seemed truly dedicated.

The lackluster fight bored the crowd as well. They grew restless, and people began having conversations rather than staying focused on the ring. Junior managed to wear down his opponent to a technical knockout. Well, it might not have been the most exciting fight, but at least Junior won. And didn't get hurt.

Junior stalked out of the ring. Ambrose approached him and whispered something into his ear. From Junior's reaction, it didn't look like Ambrose was giving him words of encouragement.

"Sorry I'm late," Jed said, dropping into the seat beside Gunny.

"What's wrong?" Gunny asked. For a man just released from jail, Jed was tense, agitated. "Did something happen with your case?"

"No, nothing like that. Mrs. Wright called just before I left. Delia's gone missing."

Gunny smiled. "Delia's done that before."

"Mrs. Wright hasn't seen her all day. And it's getting late."

Now Gunny grew concerned. "You're right. Delia wouldn't stay out so late. She knows not to worry her mother that way."

"Besides, where would a young girl want to be at this time of night?" Jed asked.

Gunny looked back to the ring. "Come on, she may be at my apartment. She's done that before."

The two men stood to leave just as the bell sounded for the next bout. Gunny glanced at Junior as he re-entered the ring. Now his face was full of fury. Whatever had been bothering him was going to be expressed through his gloves. Even the crowd sensed this was going to be a much more intense, more exciting fight.

The two fighters touched gloves. Junior held his hands in front of his face but didn't move. His opponent's fist flung out and Junior fell off balance. He landed in the ropes. The crowd went wild.

"Coming?" Jed pressed.

"Hang on." Something was wrong. Why wasn't Junior fighting back?

Junior pulled himself back up but barely defended himself. He allowed the other fighter to pummel him, smack him, dominate him. It was as if Junior didn't care. As if—

It locked into Gunny's brain like tumblers in a combination lock. *Junior is throwing the fight, just like the jockey.*

This fight had Ambrose's dirty fingers all over it.

But how could Ambrose get Junior to throw a fight? The kid loved the game. Losing wasn't going to help him reach his dream of going pro.

Junior landed flat on his back. The referee began the count.

Gunny's blood ran cold.

Delia.

Thirteen

Delia isn't at my hotel," Gunny told Jed. "Ambrose has her."

Jed stared at Gunny. "What?"

"No time to explain! We have to follow Junior."

"Which way did he go?" Jed asked.

Gunny was relieved Jed simply trusted him and didn't stop to ask questions. "Through that door," Gunny said. "Where does it lead?"

"The alley," Jed said. "Come on!"

Outside, clouds passed in front of the moon, making the night dark and moody. Gunny could just make out a shadowy figure running quickly up the street. "There!" Gunny hissed.

Jed and Gunny raced after Junior. He took a sharp turn around the corner up ahead.

Jed and Gunny arrived at the corner a moment later. Junior had vanished.

"How could we have lost him?" Jed panted. He bent over, hands on his knees to catch his breath.

Gunny also felt winded from the sprint, but he turned in a slow circle, searching for any sign of Junior. Then he realized where they were standing: in front of Ambrose Jackson's building site.

"I don't think we did." He pointed to the chicken wire that kept the neighborhood kids from sneaking into the site. It was pulled away from its posts. Just enough for a teenage boy to slip through.

"Ambrose had to stop work until he could pay his bills," Gunny told Jed. "This would make a perfect place to stash a hostage."

Gunny pried the chicken wire farther away from the post. He held it out so that Jed could squeeze in. Jed skidded on the rubble that covered the unfinished floor, sending bits of plaster and rock skittering as he went down. "Yeow!" Jed cried.

Gunny pushed through the small gap and found Jed on the ground, wincing in pain and clutching his ankle.

"What happened?" Gunny whispered.

Suddenly a movement in the corner caught Gunny's attention.

The dim glow from the streetlights outside lit an unwelcome sight: Junior holding a gun aimed straight at him.

"Stay back or I'll shoot you!" Junior shouted.

Gunny put his hands in the air. "We're not here to hurt you, Junior. You know that."

Junior's hand was shaking. "No, you're here to stop me, and that's not going to happen."

Gunny took a step forward. "Stop you from doing what?"

"I mean it! Stay back!"

"We just want to understand what's going on," Gunny said.

Junior looked at Jed on the ground, then back to Gunny. He licked his lips nervously.

"It was Ambrose, wasn't it?" Gunny asked. "He forced you to throw that fight so he could make a lot of money."

Junior nodded, looking miserable. "He took Delia. He said he'd kill her if I didn't throw the fight."

"We know."

Junior swallowed and seemed to renew his strength. "But I realized—he's not going to keep his promise. So I'm here to kill him."

"Nobody is killing nobody!" Gunny shouted. "Give me the gun, Junior!"

A sound from above made both Junior and Gunny look up.

Gunny tensed. Was that Ambrose and his goons? They could have been up there all along.

The knocking sound came again.

"That's Delia!" Junior cried. "Our code!"

"Go get her," Jed said from the floor.

"Let's get you into a hiding place," Gunny said. "Help me, Junior."

Junior slipped the gun into the back of his pants and helped move Jed out of sight. As soon as they'd pulled him behind a pallet of stacked pipes, they dashed up a nearby set of cement stairs to a level that was partly completed. Floors were laid radiating outward from the stairs, but in many places only the supports were in place. Steel girders led out to beams that extended past the building's walls. Piles of tile, tubs of plaster, sacks of cement, and sheets of drywall were stacked around.

One area seemed more finished than most. It had real walls and even a door. Junior and Gunny looked at each other, and both knew to run straight to it.

Before Gunny could stop him, Junior flung open the door.

"Delia!" he cried.

Delia sat tied to a chair, her mouth covered with tape, but luckily, she was alone.

Junior ripped the tape from her mouth. "Yeow!" she yelped.

"Are you all right?" Gunny asked as he untied her.

Delia nodded. "I heard you shouting so I knew there couldn't be any of the bad guys around. So I knocked out our code with the chair legs."

Junior grabbed her in a bear hug.

"You are one smart little lady," Gunny said.

"I'm so glad you're all right," Junior said. "I'd never forgive myself—"

They all froze.

They were no longer alone. Someone—*several someones*—were downstairs.

FOURTEEN

We're trapped," Junior said.

"We have to get out of this room, or we will be," Gunny said.

Gunny, Junior, and Delia dashed out of the room. "How will we get down?" Delia whispered. "They'll see us if we use the stairs."

"The elevator shaft!" Gunny said.

"But there's no elevator," Junior hissed.

"Who needs an elevator?" Gunny said with false bravado. He had no idea how he was going to get them down safely, but Junior and Delia were counting on him.

He peered down into the shaft. The metal sleeve had been installed and the sides were sleek. Nothing to grip there. He glanced around and spotted a coil of rope. He wasn't sure how strong it was, but it would have to do.

He raced over to the rope and wrapped an end around one of the exposed beams, tying several strong knots. He yanked hard. The knots would hold even if the rope didn't. It was a start.

He uncoiled the line as he raced back over to the shaft, then dropped it down. It didn't reach all the way, but it would get them close enough to the ground.

Junior sat at the edge of the shaft, about to go down the rope when Gunny stopped him. "Let me test it first."

There were voices now on the stairs. The gangsters were heading their way.

"No time!" Junior disappeared down into the shaft.

The sudden weight made the rope go taut, but it held. Gunny guided the rope to keep Junior from smacking into the metal sleeve of the shaft. Junior quickly made it down.

"Climb on," Gunny told Delia. He knelt down so she could wrap her arms around his neck and hang on his back.

He gripped the rope and slid over the side, just as the first of the gangsters reached their floor. He hoped the gangsters didn't spot the rope, but with all the materials strewn about, he thought they might not notice. At least, not right away.

Gunny clutched the rope and planted his feet against the shaft walls, trying to take some of his weight off the line. Delia gripped his neck so tightly he was afraid she'd strangle him, but he didn't want her to slip. Even so, her body dangled and swung as he moved down the shaft, keeping him off balance.

Then he felt his load lighten.

His heart caught and his head whipped around to look for the girl.

Panic turned to relief as he saw that Junior had reached up and grabbed her, and they'd made it safely down to the ground. Now they just had to make it out of the building.

Gunny ran over to where they had hidden Jed. "You okay?" he whispered.

Jed looked pale, but he nodded. Gunny worried that perhaps more than his ankle had broken.

"We have to get you to a hospital," Gunny said. With Junior's help he should be able to carry Jed out of the site and into a taxi.

"Where's Junior?" Delia whispered.

Gunny turned and peered into the dark space. She was right. Junior was gone.

He'd gone in pursuit of Ambrose.

"Delia, you go for the police. I'll stay here and make sure Junior and Jed are okay."

Delia looked uncertain.

"It's the most important job of all," Gunny told her. "Hurry! Get them here as quick as you can."

Delia gave a sharp nod and ran out of the construction site.

"One child safe, one more to go," Gunny muttered.

He dashed back up the stairs and stumbled to a stop. Junior had pulled Ambrose onto one of the beams jutting out beyond the edge of the building. There was nothing but the night sky behind them. Junior held the gun to Ambrose's head. Which explained why the two thugs stood backed up against a wall.

"Junior," Gunny said evenly. "Think about what you're doing."

"I know exactly what I'm doing!" Junior raged. "I'm getting a confession out of this good-for-nothing."

Ambrose licked his lips. Fear obviously made his mouth dry. "Calm down, sonny boy—"

"Don't call me that," Junior snapped.

"All right, all right."

"Confess!" Junior insisted.

"Yes! I did it. I killed your father."

"But why?" Junior moaned.

"To send a message to Marvin, who was in much deeper."

Junior's face quivered. Gunny couldn't tell if the boy was about to weep or explode. Probably a little of both.

"You killed my father!" Junior said, his words a stream of barely contained rage. "You terrified my mother and my sister. You were probably planning to kill Delia and me! You have to die."

Junior cocked the gun.

"Wait!" Gunny shouted. He wanted to talk Junior out of this, but he knew the moment Junior faltered, the gangsters would shoot. How to get them out of this alive?

"Send your goons away," Gunny told Ambrose. "Then we can all have a talk."

"We're not leaving the boss—"

"Go," Ambrose ordered. "Don't want to make the boy more nervous . . ."

Reluctantly the gangsters began to move. "You stay where I can see you," Gunny told them. "Or I'll tell Junior to shoot Ambrose myself. Head downstairs. In plain sight. Shouldn't be too hard with all that open space and no floor."

Gunny waited until the goons had placed themselves

where he'd asked. He knew they weren't out of the woods yet—with all the open areas, they could easily still shoot, but at least they would have a tougher time hitting Junior.

"So, we good?" Ambrose asked nervously. "You gonna let me go back over to that nice floor over there where there's a wall?"

"Shut up!" Junior shouted. ""You're never going anywhere again!"

"Junior, listen to me," Gunny said calmly, taking tiny steps along the beam toward Junior. "Your dad didn't want you hanging around with Ambrose because it was a mistake he made himself. It was because of Ambrose that your father got himself into trouble."

"Another reason to kill him!" Junior said.

"No!" Gunny inched forward. He stepped onto the girder. *Don't look down,* he told himself. He couldn't help it. The gangsters on the floor below peered up, shocked expressions on their faces.

Gunny wrested his eyes from the floor below and forced himself to sound calm, as if balancing on a twelve-inch beam stories above the street were something he did every day. "Don't let Ambrose force you into making bad choices. Don't let Ambrose turn you into someone like *him*. Someone who settles scores and kills without thinking."

Another step closer. Another step. Another.

"Let the cops handle this," Gunny continued. "We all heard the confession. It's over for Ambrose. Your life is just starting—don't let Ambrose steal it from you."

He was only an arm's length from Junior and Ambrose now.

"Be the man your father knew you could be."

Junior wavered. His arm slowly lowered. He looked down at the gun in his hand. He looked up at Gunny.

Then he handed Gunny the gun.

The moment he did, there was a movement below. The gangsters were pulling out their weapons!

Gunny crouched on the beam, gripped an edge for balance, and took aim.

But he couldn't pull the trigger. The same as when he'd been in the army. He just couldn't shoot!

With frustrated fury he hurled the gun as hard as he could into the stack of aluminum pipes stored beside the gangsters. The impact knocked the lightweight pipes out of their stack. They spilled out all over the floor, knocking over the gangsters.

Sirens suddenly wailed. Ambrose's head whipped around at the sound, and it threw him off balance.

"Yeeeah!" he shrieked. His arms windmilled as he struggled to keep his balance.

"No!" Junior reached out to grab Ambrose.

"Junior!" Gunny cried.

It all seemed to happen in slow motion, but Gunny knew it was only a matter of seconds.

Ambrose fell backward off the beam. Junior stumbled as he tried to save him and fell face forward onto the beam, then lost his grip and dangled over the side. Gunny lurched toward Junior, landing on his stomach, and gripped Junior's ankles.

And felt himself being dragged closer and closer to the end of the beam.

Fifteen

Gunny lay on his stomach and bent his left leg. He hooked his knee around the beam. His right leg shot out and pressed into the side of the next girder over. He managed to stop sliding. Now he just had to hang on to Junior's scrawny ankles long enough to get the boy back up onto the beam.

"Grab something!" Gunny shouted. "Anything!"

He could feel the boy shaking. Or maybe *Gunny* was the one quivering. Every muscle burned; even the cold steel seemed to burn his face where his skin pressed into the metal.

Some of the pressure eased. Junior must have found something to hang on to.

Which meant he wasn't holding on to Ambrose.

Slowly, so slowly, Gunny edged himself backward along the beam. Down on the floor below he could see police officers swarming around the gangsters. He didn't dare risk calling for help—expanding his lungs to yell seemed too dangerous. It could flip him right off the beam.

Now Junior was helping to push. Like strange snakes, they slithered backward in a long thin line. Gunny felt his legs hit a platform. He had reached the edge of the installed flooring.

He lifted up slightly and slid onto it, never releasing Junior's ankles. Then he sat back on his knees and pulled Junior the rest of the way to safety. They fell away from the edge, sprawling on the unfinished floor.

"We did it," he told the terrified boy.

"I tried to—he just went—," Junior stammered.

"I know, son. I know," Gunny said. "But you see? You tried to save him. Even after all that. You're no killer. You did great."

Junior gave Gunny a weary smile. "You're pretty impressive for an old guy."

Gunny returned the smile—with an equal amount of exhaustion. "You're not so bad yourself. For a kid. Your sister, too. " He slung an arm around Junior's shoulders. "Now let's go take care of Jed."

"You really were something," Jed said as he and Gunny waited for the doctors to sign his release papers. One ankle was wrapped and his other leg was in a cast, but other than the broken bones, he was fine. He was a little dopey from the painkillers, though.

"It was those kids," Gunny admitted. "You were right. They did have a lot to offer."

"You handled a lot," Jed said. "You really are ready."

"Ready for what?" Gunny asked.

"I'm getting too old for this," Jed continued, as if

he hadn't heard Gunny's question. "It's time to pass the torch."

"What are you talking about?" Gunny laughed. "You sure those were just painkillers they gave you?"

"This whole thing . . . all of your life . . . it's been leading here." Jed's voice was vague and sleepy. "To this moment."

"You should rest," Gunny said. "It's been quite the day."

"No, no," Jed insisted, trying to rouse himself. "There are some things you need to know."

"Not tonight," Gunny said.

"Maybe not," Jed said. "Tomorrow. But promise me you'll keep an open mind."

"Don't I always?" Gunny said with a smile.

Gunny got a lot of strange looks when he appeared for work in his crisp bellman's uniform the next morning. The bruises, cuts, and burns were in definite contrast to his usual professional and dapper style.

"Don't ask," he growled at Dodger before the boy could speak.

The little bell on the front desk jangled. A tall man with a suitcase stood waiting, smiling.

"Welcome to the Manhattan Tower Hotel," Gunny greeted the new guest. "I'll take these to your room."

"Thank you," the man said.

They rode the elevator in silence, Gunny horribly self-conscious about the condition of his face. It wasn't the impression he liked to give hotel guests.

He opened the door to the man's suite and placed

the suitcase on the luggage rack. "Will that be all, sir?"

"Actually, Gunny," the man said, "I'd like you to stay."

Gunny looked at the man sharply. "How do you know my name?"

"I'll get to that," the man said with a smile. "My name's Press. And I have a lot to tell you."

SPADER

ONE

"Hobey-ho, mates! We did it!" Vo Spader grinned at the group of smiling Aquaneer Academy cadets around him. He and his classmates were gathered on the forward dock near the academy entry port. "No more tests, rules, or Master Simmons's spot safety checks! We graduate tomorrow!"

"Aquaneers all!" the group cheered.

"Aquaneers all!" Spader repeated. With a whoop he cannonballed into the water in front of the dock. Several others dove in after him.

Spader burst through the surface and shook his head, spraying water from his long dark hair. He felt great—pumped and ready for anything. His parents were arriving on the ferry soon for the graduation ceremony tomorrow, and he couldn't wait to see them.

He pulled himself back up out of the water and sprawled on the deck, warming himself in the sun. The kids who had stayed on the dock were talking about the future.

"I'm going to Crasker," Min Chester, a girl from his Hydrotech class was saying. "My sister works at one of the Watsu ship-building facilities there." Their classmate, Per Watsu, was the son of the head of Watsu Shipyards.

"Sounds spiff," Spader said. "I'm off to Grallion."

Dor Jinsen whistled. "That's the big agro habitat. They'll put you to work there."

"Bring it on!" Spader said, leaping to his feet. "I'm ready!"

Spader had thought hard about which of the habitats dotting Cloral he'd choose after graduating. It was a big decision since each was devoted to a specific industry. He was thrilled when he got his first-choice placement.

"What are you looking forward to the most?" Min asked the group.

"My mom's cooking!" Dor said. "I'm sick of the academy menu."

"Something new to do," Spader said. "After drilling everything so many times, even this obstacle course is easy-o." He nodded toward the other side of the dock where they'd spent hours navigating the obstacle course on their water sleds. "I could do it blindfolded."

"I'd like to see you try!" Per Watsu challenged.

Spader turned to see Per Watsu above them, hanging over the rail of the observation deck. The guy was a right sinker, always bringing the mood down and trying to prove he was best at everything, especially anything Spader did well. Worse, he never seemed to have any fun. When Spader competed, he and his opponent generally had a good laugh afterward. Per was as sore a winner as he was a loser.

Per waved a hand in disgust. "I guess you just don't want to break any rules."

"Me?" Spader scoffed. "I haven't met a rule yet that I couldn't bypass."

"Then do it," Per goaded. "Prove once and for all that you're better on the course than I am."

"I already proved that," Spader said, starting to get mad. "I've beaten your standings every time."

Per's jaw set and Spader knew he'd hit a nerve. Sure, they were only seconds apart in the finals, but seconds mattered as an aquaneer, and Spader had been named First Standing over Per. Still, using the course unsupervised was strictly forbidden. And blindfolded?

"Spader doesn't care about any of that!" Dor argued. "I bet twenty grentons that he can get through it."

"I'll take that bet," Min said laughing. "I don't think he'll make it to the chute."

"No way!" Now all the kids were chattering and betting on how far through the course Spader could get. "The mama ramp will stop him!"

"Hobey!" Spader exclaimed. "I'll make it over the baby, the mama, and the papa ramps like water over a fall!"

Per smiled smugly. "Well?" he asked. "Are you going to stand by your words? Or are you going to show everyone here that you're just talk."

"Why not?" Spader grinned at the group. "What can they do? Expel me? I've already passed!"

The group let out a cheer. Per glanced at his watch, smiled, then went over to Min. "May I?" he asked, pointing at the sash she wore around her waist.

"For the cause," she quipped. She unwrapped the sash and handed it to Per.

Per tied the blindfold slowly and ceremoniously around Spader's eyes. He led him to the obstacle course entrance.

This could be a tum-tigger, Spader realized as he plunged into the water. It took him a moment to orient himself, then he struggled to unhitch the sled. His classmates on the dock shouted instructions. "The clip is on the other side." "Don't ride it into the dock!"

Once he was positioned properly at the water sled, Spader's confidence kicked back in. He'd spent so much time on the nifty little thing it felt like an extension of his limbs. He could do this!

The water sled hummed to life. The kids on the dock were now chanting: "Go Spader Go!"

He zoomed up and over the first ramp—the one they all called "baby." He slowed slightly. This wasn't about beating the clock he reminded himself, the way it was in trials. This was about getting through it.

He visualized the course. Up first were the turns. He leaned hard left and then quickly hard right. His foot grazed the cone but he made it. He couldn't celebrate the victory yet, though. He had three more turns to make— if his memory was right.

After the turns came . . . what? "Whoah!" He suddenly jolted forward. His grip must have tightened on the controls, making the sled speed up. He felt the sled angle sharply upward. He was already at the mama ramp!

"Whooo-ee!" Spader whooped as he picked up air

underneath him. He shifted his weight and hit the water hard, but maintained his balance.

He could hear cheers from the dock and smiled, knowing Per must be fuming. Halfway there!

He took in a deep breath and submerged. He needed to make it through the reef fast—he didn't have on an air globe!

No one had bothered to remind him—everyone was too wrapped up in getting on the blindfold to remember, including Spader.

He slowed the sled so he could feel his way along the reef—better to have to resurface for air than to smash into rough and sharp coral. He found the first opening and maneuvered through it, then carefully ˙ in and out of the rocky obstacle. His lungs felt as if they were going to explode any moment.

He cleared the length of the reef. *Done!* He burst back up to the surface and took in a huge gulp of air. He pictured the rest of the course. *Okay, papa ramp next, then—*

"Vo Spader, return to dock immediately."

Uh-oh . . . That order came through loud and clear over the speaker. He knew that tone only too well.

"Vo Spader, return to the dock immediately, or be removed."

Busted.

Spader pulled back on the throttle and whipped off his blindfold.

He slowly turned the sled around and saw the very unwelcome sight of Master Simmons standing on the dock, surrounded by a group of adults. Parents and alumni, no doubt, all here for the graduation ceremony tomorrow.

Time for a reckoning, Spader thought. *They can't expel me*, he told himself, but worried that maybe they actually could.

He tried to read the master's expression as he approached the dock. Oooh, not good. In fact, everyone was glaring at him. He slowed the sled, delaying the inevitable, hoping he'd come up with the perfect thing to say.

Hang on, he thought. *They've stopped looking at me, they're looking out to the open waters beyond.* He frowned. They didn't look annoyed. They looked . . . shocked.

A loud boom nearly startled him off the sled. *What the—*

Spader craned his neck to see two vessels just beyond the academy water gates. One was the ferry carrying the guests for graduation. The other boat was . . .

"Raiders!" he gasped.

A booming sound came again, and a body dropped off the ferry pilot's tower and plunged into the water. The sea pirates were firing on the ferry!

TWO

Ear-piercing sirens screeched from the loudspeakers all across the academy. Everywhere Spader looked he saw frantic activity: aquaneers suiting up on the run, ships being launched, and people shouting instructions. But this was a training facility, not designed for military operations. Spader wondered if they'd have the means to take on armed raiders.

Then it hit him. His parents were on that ferry!

His fingers hit the throttle, and the sled zipped across the water. He zoomed out the academy gates, heading straight toward the fight.

His stomach tightened. There was blood in the water.

He gritted his teeth and urged the sled to go faster. He glanced up to check the distance, and his heart nearly stopped.

His father was out on deck—trading punches with a raider!

Spader made a sharp turn, sending up spray, and

pulled alongside the vessel. He wanted to board behind the raider. That would give him the advantage of surprise.

He leaped from his sled and grabbed the handholds on the side of the ship. He scrambled up and flung himself onto the raider's back. He shoved his arm across the raider's throat and yanked back, hard.

"Vo!" Spader's father, Benn, looked startled and then grinned. "Glad you're here, laddie!"

The raider shoved his fingers between Spader's arm and his neck. He brought his shoulder up sharply, knocking Spader's jaw.

Spader's head whipped back and his hold loosened. The raider squirmed out of his grip, but Benn Spader was on him.

"No, you don't!" Benn shouted. "Grab him!" He pushed the raider back into Spader. Spader was ready for him—he gripped the man's arms tightly.

The raider lurched and lunged, desperate to break free. He kicked out at Benn, who quickly grabbed his legs.

"Man overboard!" Spader cried.

Together he and his father hurled the raider over the rail and into the water below.

There were splashes all around the ship as raiders dropped off the boat. They swam toward their vessel.

"Was it something I said?" Spader joked.

"They didn't like the new odds," Benn said. He pointed to the academy boats heading their way.

"I think they just didn't want to have to face Benn Spader and son!"

"Come on," Benn said. "We need to check on your mum."

They hurried below. Spader saw ten parent types huddled together in the cabin. A woman with a single dramatic gray streak in her dark hair stood when they entered.

"Vo! Benn!" Ginja Spader cried.

Spader's body flooded with relief when he saw his mum. She looked frightened, but fine.

"No worries, Mum," Spader said. "All spiff here."

"What are you doing on board?" she asked, folding him into a hug.

"Just had to check up on you and Pop," Spader said.

The first of the academy aquaneers boarded, weapons at the ready.

Benn held up a hand. "We're all under control down here."

"There weren't very many of them," one of the other parents added.

"They seemed to know that tomorrow is graduation day," Ginja Spader said.

The aquaneer nodded and reholstered his weapon. "Makes sense. Hit the boat carrying parents, knowing they'd probably be bringing gifts and grentons with them."

"They—they got some of the pilot's crew," Benn said.

"That's how they usually operate," the aquaneer said gravely. "Is everyone all right here? Anyone need medical attention?"

After organizing the few people with injuries, the aquaneer crew went up to the pilot house to bring the ship in. Soon they were safely arriving at the academy. Everyone on the dock let out a cheer.

Spader gave a big wave and hopped onto the dock. He was instantly surrounded by his friends, thumping him on the back and congratulating him. Min raced up to her parents and disappeared into their arms.

A man strode over to Spader and stuck out his beefy hand. "Well done, mate. Nice to see a young person showing such courage and initiative."

"Thanks," Spader said.

"I'm Chi Watsu," the man said.

Aha, Spader thought. *Per's father.* Per was a shorter, slimmer version.

"If you ever need a job, there's always a place in my shipyard. We need motivated young people like you."

Behind Mr. Watsu, Spader saw Per glowering.

"Too bad my own son doesn't show such initiative," Chi Watsu added. "Maybe then he'd—"

Before Mr. Watsu could finish the thought, an announcement came over the loudspeaker.

"Vo Spader, please report to the dean's office. Immediately."

Mr. Watsu gave Spader a light punch on the arm. "Must be about giving you a commendation."

Spader smiled weakly. That hadn't sounded like a "come on in and get a medal" announcement.

THREE

"What am I going to do with you, Vo Spader?" Master Simmons demanded. "It's been this way your entire time here at the academy. You show great promise and skill, and then you do something completely foolish. Not to mention dangerous."

Spader wanted to say that his skill should be all that mattered, not whether or not he followed a bunch of dumb rules. But he knew enough to keep his mouth shut.

"I could expel you for using the obstacle course unsupervised." Simmons shook his head. "And you did it *blindfolded*!"

"I beat it, though," Spader blurted out. "You should have seen me! Maybe your next cadets should—"

The master shot Spader a look that made Spader instantly stop speaking.

"By the gates of Faar, what made you do such a stupid thing when you *knew* you'd be caught? Are you that intent on proving you don't have to follow the rules?"

"What do you mean?" Spader asked.

"The parents' tour!" the master said. "It was on all of your schedules for the day."

"Oh, right . . ." Spader hadn't actually read the schedule, but he was certain Per had. Spader's ears grew hot with anger. The timing was too perfect—Per had set him up to be caught.

"Under normal circumstances I would expel you," Master Simmons continued. "But those parents out there view you as a hero." The Master sighed and rubbed his face. "Another foolhardy move. You went into a dangerous situation without knowing the facts. You put yourself and possibly others at risk."

"My parents were aboard that vessel," Spader protested. "I had to do something."

"I know. I'm not saying it wasn't also courageous." He shook his head. "That's why you've been such a difficult student. You can be selfless and brave, but you just don't think!"

"Please let me graduate," Spader said. "I promise to start thinking more."

The master looked as if he were fighting back a smile. "I certainly hope so. You're a good lad, Vo. People like having you around. Just don't make them regret putting up with your recklessness. Like I'm about to do."

"Thank you!" Spader said. He grabbed the master's hand and gave it a hard shake. "I'll make you and the academy proud. You'll see!"

"I have high hopes," the master said. "Dismissed."

Spader hurried out of the office. He knew his parents were waiting for him back at his room, but first he needed to have a word or two with Per. Loud and choice words.

He didn't have to go far. Per was sitting on the dock rail as if he were waiting for Spader to come out of the master's office.

"You set me up," Spader said. "You knew exactly when the master would be at the obstacle course."

Per shrugged. "You could have said no. But as usual you had to impress everybody. The great and daring Vo Spader at it again. You never take anything seriously."

"Fighting off the raiders was pretty serious," Spader retorted. "What did you do? Run to daddy."

Per's eyes flashed with anger. "You didn't go into that fight to help. It was just showing off." He gave a nasty laugh. "You probably thought it would be fun! It's all just a big game to you."

Spader's fist connected with Per's jaw. Startled, Per fell to the ground. Spader was startled too—he hadn't realized he was going to hit Per until he saw his hand fly out.

Per scrambled up to his feet and swung. Spader ducked the blow, but Per was fast and came back in with a punch to Spader's midsection.

"Oof." Spader doubled over. As Per came at him again, he twisted and kicked out in a sweeping roundhouse, knocking Per back to the ground.

Per leaped up again with an angry shout and flung himself onto Spader. The sudden, sideways weight knocked Spader off balance. They toppled off the dock and into the water.

Water rushed up Spader's nose, and he wished he

were wearing an air globe. He kicked hard and resurfaced quickly, but he felt Per grab his legs, making it impossible for him to swim away.

Spader squirmed and wriggled but he couldn't break free. Per suddenly yanked hard, dunking Spader under.

Spader shot back up, but Per was instantly on him again, grabbing a handful of his long hair. Spader's head jerked back, and Per pulled his head under the water. Spader scissored his legs around Per's, then tossed him sideways, breaking the boy's hold. Spader kicked hard to put distance between them. Per grabbed Spader's feet in a viselike grip and pulled him down under again.

Is he trying to kill me? Without air globes, Per would drown himself right along with Spader. Per didn't seem to care.

Spader felt as if he were suffocating. He stopped thinking about trading blows with Per anymore—he needed to get to the surface. But Per kept at it, weighing Spader down.

Something dropped into the water nearby. A pair of powerful hands yanked the two boys apart. Per tumbled away, and Spader shot up to the surface. He took in big, grateful gulps of air.

Per's head popped up a few feet away.

"You trango fish!" Spader yelled. He raised his arms to stroke toward Per, but a strong hand grabbed his wrist, holding him back.

"Stop. This minute," Benn Spader ordered his son. "Back to the dock. Now."

Spader slowly swam back to the dock, weighed down by embarrassment. To have to be rescued by his dad.

And his father didn't seem too happy about it either.

Spader glanced up at the dock. A group of parents had watched the whole thing. Spader saw his mum's disappointed expression. He could kick himself for getting into a fight in front of everyone. He should have waited until he and Per were alone.

Spader pulled himself out of the water and stood dripping on the dock, waiting for his father. Per climbed up a few feet away.

Spader watched Per's father storm over to Per. He grabbed Per's arm and dragged him down the dock. "You let that boy catch you off guard?" the older Watsu demanded. "Then you had to be rescued by his father?"

"He didn't rescue me!" Per shouted. "I was winning."

"*Winning!*" Spader sputtered. His fists clenched. He wanted to finish the fight—show Per once and for all who would have won.

"Stop it. Now," Benn Spader ordered.

Ginja Spader joined her husband and son. "Are you all right?" she asked.

"Fine," Spader said, looking down at his feet.

"No, you're not fine," Benn said. "You're so caught up in anger and adrenaline you're not thinking straight."

Spader gaped at his father. "That's not true! Per—"

"Let's go to your room," Benn said, cutting him off.

Spader knew better than to protest. He took his mum's overnight case, and they walked to Spader's room in silence.

Spader was fuming. First Per got him into trouble with the master and now this.

When they arrived at his room, Benn told Ginja, "Give us some time."

"Of course," Ginja replied. "I'll go to the visitors' quarters. I need to freshen up." She gave them a wry smile. "Not as badly as you two need to do, of course." She took her case back from her son and left them alone.

The warm day had dried their clothes a bit. Spader handed his father a towel.

"Vo, you're a good, smart, and talented lad," Benn said, toweling off his hair.

"But . . ." Spader said, knowing that this compliment was just the beginning of a lecture.

"You seem to have no control. No discipline."

"I get the job done," Spader protested. "No one is better in the water than I am."

"That may be true," his father conceded, "but that's not enough. By far."

Spader sighed. He'd heard this one before. But this time his father seemed much more intense about it.

"Hitting that boy," Benn said, shaking his head. "How was that 'getting the job done'?"

Spader looked away. When his father saw his final academy report, he'd only be angrier—it had the same kinds of criticisms. "Not living up to his full potential" was also a comment that his parents wouldn't be happy to see.

"You jeopardized a career that hasn't even begun," his dad continued. "Do you want to be known as a brawler?"

"Per had it coming!" Spader protested.

Exasperated, Benn threw his hands into the air. "Even now! You don't see it! That momentary satisfaction of hitting someone who insulted you doesn't make up for the damage you cause yourself."

"He set me up!" Spader fumed. "He knew the master would be passing by, and that's when he dared me to—"

Benn held up a hand. "Stop right there. Do you hear yourself? He dared you to do something that was against the rules, not to mention dangerous. All you're angry about is that he did it in a way that you'd be caught. What do you care if he dares you to do something?"

Spader's mouth dropped open. He didn't have a good answer to that.

"You sound just as angry now as you must have been when you took a swing at him," his father said. "You have to let it go. Anger has a bad habit of festering and getting worse."

"You're right," Spader finally conceded. "I'll let it go. Besides, after graduation tomorrow I won't have to see his smug face again!"

Benn shook his head. "I have a feeling this is something we're going to have to keep talking about."

FOUR

Wishing you smooth waters, the strength of the waves, and the wisdom of the Faarians for this next phase of your life!"

Spader beamed as his friends and family toasted him. His parents were throwing him a going-away party; tomorrow he'd start his assignment on Grallion.

Spader held up his glass of sparkling graka juice. "Wisdom and strength are all very well and good," he jokingly complained. "But how about wishing me the fun of a skimmer race and the adventures of an aqua explorer!"

Benn slung an arm around his son's shoulders and grinned. "That's my boy! Always looking for excitement! Me, I just want to be sure he doesn't lose the job and have to live off his mum and me for the rest of his life!"

"You mean I won't be getting an allowance anymore?" Spader asked in mock horror. "Can I at least send home my dirty clothing?"

"You somehow managed to do it at the academy," his mother teased.

"Sure, he managed," someone in the back of the group shouted, "by never doing it! Phew, the smell!"

Everyone laughed, Spader the hardest of all.

"There's someone here I want you to meet," Benn said. He brought Spader to the refreshment table where a tall slim man stood cutting a piece of larto fruit pie. "Press, I'd like you to meet my son, Vo Spader."

"I've heard a lot about you," Press said.

"Good, I hope," Spader said.

"Definitely. I can't wait to get into the water with you," Press said. "I hear you're some skimmer scuttler."

"I make good time," Spader admitted with a grin.

"Before you go, we should have ourselves a race," Press said.

"You're on!" Spader said. "Maybe we can even get my dad into the mix."

"I'd rather watch and referee," Benn said. "With you two, someone has to be sure you're playing by the rules."

"Do you work with my father?" Spader asked.

"No," Benn said.

"Not exactly," Press said at the same time.

Spader's forehead wrinkled. "Which is it?" he asked, confused.

"Both," Press answered quickly. "I've been traveling all over Cloral, visiting the different habitats. Your father was kind enough to get me temporary work with him."

"Press isn't around very often, so I thought I'd invite him to join us for your party," Benn added.

Spader studied Press. He seemed like a decent sort, and his father obviously thought highly of him. So he wondered why his father had never mentioned him before.

"Press and I met right after you left to start your training at the academy," Benn said, as if he'd read Spader's mind. "I'm sure you'll be running into each other now and again."

"So, you're off to a new habitat tomorrow?" Press said.

"Sure am," Spader said. "I'd be happy being an aquaneer just about anywhere, but Grallion was my first choice. It's a spiff assignment."

"You're lucky it wasn't taken away from you after your behavior that last day at the academy," Benn said.

Spader frowned at the reminder that he'd disappointed his dad. He noticed Press's glance flick quickly from him to his father. "Ahhh, school days," Press said. "Gotta admit, I got up to my own fair share of hijinx back in the day." He winked at Spader. "I bet there are stories about your dad's time back at the academy."

Spader grinned. "Yeah, old man," he teased his father. "I bet Mum has some stories to tell."

Now Benn threw his head back and laughed. "Don't get her started! I'll never be able to scold you again!" He threw an arm across Spader's shoulders and gave him a squeeze. Spader's mood instantly brightened.

"Let's take this party to the water," Spader called. "Who's up for a few spins around Point Clarion?"

A cheer went up. Everyone grabbed their globes and their gear and headed for the door.

"Should the old-timers join the next generation?" Press asked.

"Hobey!" Benn said with a grin. "Why should the young ones have all the fun?"

"What are we waiting for?" Spader said. "Let's go!"

"Welcome to Grallion!" Wu Yenza, Grallion's chief aquaneer, strode to the center of a catwalk above the loading dock where Spader and the other new recruits stood awaiting work assignments.

It was finally happening. His first day of "real life"— on his own, with an important job where he got to spend all his time on the water.

"We work hard, we work safe, and our work is for the good of Grallion. We keep things coming and going, and we take great pride in it. I expect each and every one of you to live up to the high standards and feel proud to call yourselves aquaneers."

Spader beamed; he was *already* proud to be there.

"We work in teams; there's very little we can do successfully alone. You're going to rotate through shifts and tasks in your first months here."

Wu Yenza began calling out names and teams. Spader hadn't realized there were so many crews and departments. Then he heard something he hadn't expected: Per Watsu's name.

Spader frowned. A dark cloud called Per Watsu just blotted out the bright and sunny days up ahead.

"Okay, let's start this day!" Wu Yenza declared. "Smooth waters, everyone."

Spader passed Per as he headed toward his work crew.

"I hope I get my transfer soon," Per grumbled as he walked by Spader. "I wanted to go to Prongo, but there was a waiting list."

"Hey, mate, if there's anything I can do to help hurry that transfer along, just let me know," Spader said. "I'm as eager to see you on another habitat as you are to be there."

"I was just lucky Wu Yenza wasn't there to see the mess I'd made," Kor Tradco said, laughing. "I'd have been transferred for sure!"

Spader laughed and helped himself to another plateful of grilled Kooloo fish. Tradco, another new aquaneer, lived in the flat next door to Spader's and had invited the other aquaneers on the row over for grilled fish. Spader was happy to see that Per hadn't come.

"Wu Yenza is tough," Bry Loran, one of the older aquaneers, said. "But she's fair."

"She really knows her stuff," Ara Renton, another senior aquaneer agreed. She took a swig of her graka. "When we were hit by that rogue wave, I thought we were done for. But Yenza got us through."

"We had storm training at the academy," Spader said. "They can be real tum-tiggers."

"The unpredictability," Ara said. "That's the hardest part."

"Like with raiders," Loran said. "They appear out of nowhere."

"Don't I know it," Spader said, settling beside Loran on the ground. "Raiders hit right in front of the academy the day before graduation."

"I heard there's been raider activity over near Crasker," Ara said.

Loren nodded. "Makes sense. It's foggy around Crasker—great way to sneak up on a vessel."

"They try something with me again, and they'll wish they were in the city of Faar," Spader said. "I'd make 'em vanish just as completely."

"Well, the Kooloo fish vanished," Tradco said. "Should I put another one on?"

"You have to ask?" Loran said. He held up his empty plate.

Spader lay back to watch the light changing as night approached. He sighed with contentment. Good mates, a job to be proud of, and exciting challenges ahead—and a chance to prove he really had the stuff to make a great aquaneer. This was one spiff life.

As long as Per Watsu stayed out of his way.

FIVE

Hobey!" Spader punched his fist in the air in excitement. "Real duty!"

Tradco peered over Spader's shoulder at the work rotation list posted at the aqua center. He let out a whistle. "Lucky you, mate. Loading dock. Where the action is."

During the probationary period the juniors were cycled through different departments. Once they were full aquaneers, they'd spend most of their time at the docks, but Wu Yenza wanted them to understand how their work was supported by other departments, and how what they did was critical to the smooth running of Grallion.

"What did you pull?" Spader asked.

Tradco sighed. "The alt power depot."

Spader's forehead crinkled. "What's alt power?" So far he'd been through the maintenance depot and the piloting depot, along with continued training on equipment and life-safety skills.

"Wind systems," Tradco explained. He shook his head. "Probably hasn't been used since the time of Faar, but still they make us learn how they work."

"Wind?" Spader laughed. "I guess there's a reason for it, but I can't think what. Well, you have a party, mate. I know I will!" He clapped Tradco's shoulders, then strode toward the loading docks and over to Wu Yenza, who stood studying her work sheet.

"Spader reporting, right and ready," he said.

Yenza smiled at him. "Glad you're so eager to work."

Spader grinned back. "It's what I'm here for!"

"It's what we're *all* here for," Yenza reminded him with a smile. "I've got you on escort. Today we'll have two of you working the dock here. It's a busy day. The Jorsen habitat will be coming by for supplies—that's a lot of load-out. And we've got the usual small cruisers, deliveries, and visitors to guide in. Your partner is also a junior, but there will be senior staff around too. If you run into trouble."

"We won't!" Spader assured her.

"Good. Here comes your partner now."

Spader turned and his grin froze.

A sweet plum day just turned sour. He was paired with Per Watsu.

Clearly Per wasn't overjoyed to see Spader, either.

Wu Yenza frowned. "Is there a problem here?" she asked.

"No, no problem," Per said.

"Good to hear. Now let's get to work. Smooth waters."

"Smooth waters," Per and Spader replied.

Per and Spader headed toward the dock where they'd sign out their skimmers. They gave their names to the worker who was checking out the equipment for the shift.

"Stay out of my way, Spader," Per snarled while they waited.

"Isn't that kind of the job?" Spader teased. "To be sure everyone stays out of everyone else's way?"

The dockmen checking out their skimmers snickered. Per glared.

"I mean it," Per snapped. "Steer clear." He put on his air globe. As a safety measure everyone wore buoyancy compensator belts and globes, even though they were working above water.

"I always do," Spader said. "But I have to say, I'm a little hurt. I was hoping we could work up a synchronized skimmer routine for Wu Yenza."

Now the other workers in the area began to listen.

"I can see it now," Spader said, enjoying the ridiculous image of performing with Per on skimmers. "We can start by crisscrossing a few times. Then we come to a sharp stop and do ever-widening circles. Can't you see it?"

The other workers obviously could. They were all smiling and laughing.

"We should find out what her favorite music is and choreograph—"

"Are you capable of being serious?" Per's face was growing red with frustration. "Everything's always one big joke to you."

"Not everything," Spader retorted. "Just you."

"Ooh, got you there," someone called out.

"Get to work, Per. Why are you dawdling?" Spader hopped aboard his skimmer and peeled out, leaving Per in his wake.

"Slow down, young man!" a supervising aquaneer called to him from a nearby skimmer. "It's not a race!"

Spader gave the woman a nod and a wave, and pulled back on the throttle. It *was* a race, only he and Per were the only ones who knew. *And I just won!* Spader gloated inwardly.

Once Per arrived at the marking buoy that established the perimeter Spader and he would be patrolling, the aquaneer supervising their area gave them their instructions. They were expecting a habitat to arrive. While the more senior staff would attend to the habitat, Per and Spader would escort the smaller ships in. Until then, they were to direct the usual vessels loading and unloading, and keep traffic running smoothly.

"It's important you two stay in synch. We want to move quickly to keep everyone happy, but smartly, to keep everyone safe. Be aware of each other."

Spader and Per exchanged a look. "Oh, I'd say we're aware of each other," Spader said with a smirk.

"Whether we want to be or not," Per muttered.

Spader spotted a mid-size ship approaching the perimeter buoys. "I'm on it!" he declared.

"No, I am." Per zipped in front of Spader, cutting him off.

Spader gaped after him.

"Your mate has initiative," the aquaneer commented. "You take the next one."

"He's not my mate," Spader said, "but if he wants to

play that way, I'm game." He quickly angled the skimmer toward another arriving vessel.

"Hobey, mates!" he called up to the people on board the cruiser. "I'm Spader, your Grallion welcoming committee!"

"Nice to meet you, lad," the man on deck said with a grin. "Let's take this in."

"Sweet and smooth," Spader said. *And faster than Per,* he thought. "Let's give it some zip," he said. "Best way to not get stuck behind a plugger."

Spader took off at a quick clip, using his minispeaker to call back instructions to the pilot navigating through the busy waters. He glanced in Per's direction. Excellent. A vessel towing a platform was crossing right in front of Per and the ship he was guiding. They were going to have to wait.

Spader kept his eyes peeled for traffic, but it was clear all the way in. As he was leaving the docking zone, he passed Per. "Even giving you a head start I beat you," Spader said.

Per ignored him and Spader laughed. He had just brought in his first vessel and showed up Per at the same time. *Pretty nice.*

Spader passed a small craft that didn't seem to be going anywhere. He went over to find out what was going on. "Not a good place to park," he said.

"I can't figure out why it's stalled," the woman at the controls said.

"Hang on, maybe I can help."

He stopped the skimmer and dove below. He instantly saw the problem. Somehow she had gotten kelp in the intake, cutting off the supply of water that powered the engines.

He reached into his water boot and pulled out his trusty knife. It was a beaut—large, with a silver handle. His father had given it to him as a graduation present. Now he used it to cut away some kelp.

He resurfaced and held up the strands. "Got your culprit right here."

The woman frowned. "I should have checked after I went through that patch on the way in. It's an old system. It's not self-regulating like the newer models."

"I'll get you a tow," Spader suggested. "It would be a natty-do if the kelp tangled farther up into the works. I can't do a serious cleanout here."

"Thanks." The woman looked relieved. "It's embarrassing sitting here tying up traffic."

"Just pretend you're keeping watch on everyone," Spader said with a wink. "Make 'em think you're here supervising. Like this." He scrambled back up onto the skimmer and draped the offending kelp over the handles. He gave a little nod to a passing vessel. "Keep up the good work!" he called to the pilot.

The woman laughed.

"Maybe *you* should get back to work," Per said as he cruised by.

Spader watched as Per zipped to the supervisor at the buoy. They spoke for a moment, and then both turned and looked at Spader. Great. Per beat him back to the buoy and was probably bad-mouthing him besides.

Spader kicked the skimmer into high gear. "Lady

needs a tow," Spader told the supervisor. "How do I get one to her?"

"I'll let them know," the supervisor said. "Good work, checking on that disabled vessel."

Per looked disgusted. Without a word he did a one-eighty and headed toward a new incoming.

"That's really your lane," the supervisor told Spader. "You need to jump to it a bit more. The crafts come in quick and can't wait around while you boys decide who's going to handle what."

Spader's jaw dropped, but then he shut it again. No sense in arguing with this guy—it was Per who was the problem.

For the rest of the afternoon Spader and Per went head-to-head over who could get to an incoming vessel faster, and then who could guide them into the docks first. They even raced back to the buoys. Very quickly they stopped bothering with lanes at all and crisscrossed the harbor, each determined to guide in the most ships.

A new vessel was coming in. Spader leaned forward, willing his skimmer to go even faster. He could see Per doing the same.

"Back off!" Per called. "This one's mine!"

"Gotta beat me to it!" Spader called back.

They were each kicking up wake, and Spader ignored the shouts and curses he heard around him as he deftly scooted by the smaller crafts making their way around the loading docks.

That spinney head, Spader thought as he and Per both raced toward the bow of the vessel. *He's not going to back down. Well, neither am I.*

"Get back to the buoy!" Per shouted, heading straight toward Spader.

"You go back," Spader said. "It's my turn!"

"There are no turns!" Per yelled. "Just the job!"

You want to play that way, fine, Spader thought. He knew any minute Per would have to change direction.

Only he didn't.

He's crazy! Spader thought, his heart racing.

At the last possible moment Spader made a sharp turn. The skimmer responded instantly and spun off out of Per's way. The sudden shift and Spader's unbalanced weight tipped the skimmer over sideways, throwing Spader into the water. The skimmer lay on its side like a misshapen buoy—right in the path of the oncoming vessel.

Six

Spader watched the collision with horrified eyes. The vessel plowed directly into the skimmer, forcing it under.

If I'd been on the skimmer . . . Spader didn't want to think about that.

The cruiser came to a stop, and a swarm of aquaneers appeared to assess the problem. Spader swam toward them, eager to help.

"Stay back," his supervisor barked.

"I'm in the water," Spader offered, "Let me go below and—"

"You've done enough already."

A rescue raft arrived. "Get in," the operator said.

"I'm fine," Spader said. "I'll swim back."

"And continue to be a danger out here? You'll do no such thing."

Thoroughly humiliated, Spader climbed into the raft. The only good thing was that Per was also being sent in. He glumly watched the senior staff bring in the vessel—the job he and Per were supposed to do.

+ + +

"No excuse," Wu Yenza declared. Her eyes flashed with anger. "An aquaneer's *only* concern is safety. Not who does it the fastest or with the most style. But who keeps the docks running smoothly and with no accidents. Instead, you two *cause* accidents."

Spader gazed down at the floor, feeling his stomach turn over.

"I've had reports that you two were in some kind of race all day," she continued. "Well, this little competition of yours nearly cost us a vessel's safe entry. It *did* cost us a skimmer. Actually"—she turned her angry eyes to Spader—"that's going to cost *you* several months' pay. Accidents happen, but this you brought on yourself."

"Understood," Spader said.

Yenza paced her office. "Give me one good reason why I shouldn't let you both go?"

Per grew pale. "I'm waiting for placement on Prongo," he said. "If I lose this position, they'll never take me."

"If you two are let go from Grallion, it's unlikely either of you will be aquaneers," Yenza said flatly.

"All I've ever wanted was to be an aquaneer like my father," Spader blurted out. "Please give me another chance! I never make the same mistake twice."

Yenza smirked. "You just keep making new ones?"

Spader couldn't help himself—he laughed. "At least I won't bore you by repeating myself."

Yenza rubbed her temples as if the situation were giving her a headache. "What am I going to do with you two?" Then she looked straight at them. "Here's how it's going to go. You are off port and dock duty. You are on

Alt-power maintenance until I decide to put you back into action."

"Yes, Yenza," the boys said in unison.

"And you will work all your shifts together," she said sternly. "You will either learn to work as a team, or you will kill each other. At this moment I truly don't know which way this will go."

Yenza couldn't have come up with a worse punishment, Spader thought. This was a right sinker.

SEVEN

Why do we need to check and repack the windworks?" Per complained for about the hundredth time. "They're never used."

"They may not have been used since the time of Faar," Spader replied, "but that's our assignment, and we're going to do it."

"Of course we're going to do it," Per snapped. "I'm not letting you get me in trouble again."

"Me?" Spader's blood boiled. How could Per—*Forget it*, he told himself. *Don't let him get to you.*

It had already been a boring, irritating week and at least fifty times a shift—maybe more—Spader had to keep himself from punching Per.

"We have one more vessel to do," Spader said. "Stop gobbing and let's get to it."

The two boys boarded the cruiser docked in the maintenance shed. Per was right, Spader conceded. Alt power didn't make much sense. Vessels all ran on the much more controllable water power. Some of the smaller vessels, however, came equipped with the ability to harness wind and had the means to do so stowed about in hidden compartments. Aquaneers needed to have basic understanding of alt power, but Spader had never known anyone who had ever actually used it.

Spader crossed the deck to open one of the compartments where the windworks were stored. Because it was considered emergency equipment, everything had to be set up by hand, as it would only go into effect if none of the automatic systems were working.

That's odd, he thought. He couldn't find the latch.

"You're looking in the wrong place," Per said.

Spader frowned. "The latches on the other boats were here."

Per strolled to the center of the deck and tripped a hidden lever that was flush with the flooring. The hatch popped open. Per smirked at Spader. "The other boats were Watsu one-twenty-four Bs. This is a Watsu one-twenty-six D."

Spader's father had spent hours teaching him about ship design, but there was no way Spader could know every detail of every vessel used on Cloral. Not like Per. Per's family *made* the vessels!

"You could have just told me," Spader fumed. He stalked to the storage compartment, and he and Per raised and secured the center mast. Then they hauled up the sails and tied off their lines. Together they practiced bringing the boom about, which, if the boat weren't tethered, would have helped them change direction.

They went through the list of required moves in

silence. Spader had found not speaking was the best tactic with Per.

As they were reloading the storage compartments, Wu Yenza strode into the shed. "Glad to see you working so well together," she said.

Per and Spader exchanged a look. Spader wouldn't call what they were doing "working well together"— more like barely tolerating each other.

"I believe you're ready for on-water work," she said.

"Spiff!" Spader exclaimed. "I mean, thank you for the opportunity."

Yenza smiled. "Most juniors aren't thrilled by wind systems. But it's a necessary facet of knowledge for all aquaneers."

"Understood," Spader said.

"There have been severe storms around Crasker," Yenza explained. "Some of their fleet has been damaged as a result, and they're short on transport boats. So rather than delivering the goods and personnel we've been expecting, they've asked if we can pick it up ourselves. You'll be part of the team making the run."

"Both of us?" Per asked.

Yenzu frowned. "Yes, both of you. Will that be a problem, Watsu?"

"No," Per said hastily. "No problem at all. Promise."

Spader had a feeling that was going to be a tough promise to keep.

"I think that's everything and everyone," the man on the Crasker loading dock called up. "You're ready to go."

The two-day trip to Crasker had been uneventful.

They had arrived on schedule, and the shipment of thermal regulators and ballast equalizers had been waiting for them. Three engineers who had designed experimental devices they planned to test on the underwater farms on Grallion had also come aboard with their equipment.

Crasker was interesting, but not really Spader's style. A habitat devoted to manufacturing, Crasker didn't have the beautiful farms and open spaces he loved on Grallion.

Or maybe it was seeing the Watsu name blazoned across so many of the buildings. Per's family manufactured many of the ships used throughout Cloral, and Crasker was one of the biggest habitats dedicated to building them. Even the cruiser they were on was a Watsu. The vessel followed the same basic design of the other ships its size: cargo holds below, living quarters in the middle, the upper deck, and then the pilot's tower. It was a fairly small vessel, carrying ten crew members, who split day and night shifts. Happily, Per and Spader, as the juniors aboard, were put on different shifts and they barely saw each other.

Once the ship had cleared the habitat, Clayton, Spader's shift supervisor, joined him at the rail. "Ready for some more drills?" Clayton asked.

"Always!" Spader replied.

"We'll do some more water sled work," Clayton said.

"I'll fetch one," Spader said, turning to head to the equipment storage below.

"Not so fast." Clayton tossed Spader a globe. "You're going to access a sled from the water."

Spader put on the globe. "I can do that?"

"You're going to try," Clayton replied, putting on an air globe so they'd be able to communicate while Spader was underwater. "Put on a harness, too."

Harnesses were stretchy cords that kept workers attached to the ship. Some were clipped onto rings on the hull; others, like the one Spader was going to wear, were attached to a winch on deck, manned by senior staff. This way a trainee in trouble could be hoisted back onto the ship.

Spader hated wearing the harness—it made him feel like a wee baby just learning to be water safe—but he knew they were required for drills while the boat was under way. He put his arms through the openings and buckled the harness belt around his waist.

"All set," Spader announced.

"This is a timed drill," Clayton explained. "In an emergency you may not have a globe with you, so it's important to work quickly. If you fell overboard, for example."

"You mean like this?" Spader slid across the deck flailing his arms. With a loud "Whooooo-ah!" he somersaulted over the rail and splashed into the water.

When he resurfaced, he saw Clayton laughing above him. "Yeah, something like that," Clayton said.

The ship was moving at a good clip, and the harness was dragging Spader with it. He swam to the hull and clutched the grips that were spaced in intervals along the sides. He placed his feet in the lower grips and leaned out, relishing the invigorating feel of the breeze and the spray. He had spent many hours riding "shipside" on his father's runs.

"Steady on?" Clayton asked.

"Like the ship and I are molded from the same piece!" Spader replied. "So what do I do?"

"The storage units in the holds can also be opened from the water. So you'll need to find the hatches that correspond with those units."

"All right," Spader said.

"Pop the hatch open and get out the sled. Keep in mind, you could need to do this without a harness, an air globe, and while the ship is moving."

"Is that all?" Spader quipped.

"I'll be here with the lines," Clayton said. He glanced at his watch. "And the timer! Go!"

Spader scooted along the hull using the hand and foot grips. He had to push against the force of the water rushing over him, but he made it pretty quickly. Now he just had to figure out how to open the hatch and pull out the sled without falling off the side of the ship, or letting in too much water.

He gazed toward the horizon. A wave was approaching. If he timed it just right . . .

Hang on . . . hang on. . . . The swell of the wave raised the ship, taking Spader with it. At the top of the crest, he quickly popped open the latch and yanked out a water sled and shut the hatch. As the boat slammed back down the back side of the wave, Spader kicked away from the ship on the water sled.

"Well done!" Clayton cheered. "Fastest time I've ever seen."

"Easy-o," Spader said.

"Now for repair drills," Clayton said.

"Slack me," Spader said. "And I'll be back in a flash."

Clayton released the entire length of the harness so that Spader could maneuver. Spader had run the same drills en route to Crasker, so he knew what to do.

He submerged the sled and zipped to each of the intake valves under the ship, which he'd inspect if he were checking for damage or maintenance. He quickly returned to his starting point and resurfaced.

Strange . . . The light had changed. Clayton stood at the rail staring up at the sky. It had grown dark and ominous.

"Come in," Clayton said. "Now."

"Should I put back the sled first?" Spader asked, guiding the sled alongside the hull. "Or carry it on board?"

Clayton's answer was drowned out by a sudden torrential downpour. A huge wave knocked Spader off the sled—and about ten wickams away from the ship. Only the harness kept him from being swept farther out.

It was hard to see with the rain pouring down, but he could just about make out Clayton struggling with the winch. He thought he could feel the harness pulling him, but it might have been the violent chop of the storm.

Another wave crashed down, but this time Spader was lucky. The undertow brought him back in line with the ship.

"Hang on," Clayton called above the howling storm.

"Doin' my best, mate!" Spader called back. The high winds and waves buffeted him around badly, wearing him down. His muscles burned as he fought the heavy, roiling water to get to the ladder.

There it was. Spader kicked hard and stretched as far as he could to grab a rung. *Yes!* He pulled himself halfway out of the water but was instantly swept off by another wave. It slammed him into the side of the boat. His body went limp and he slipped underwater.

"I'll try to lift you. Forget about the ladder!" Clayton hollered.

Spader felt himself being pulled out of the water. *Wham!* He slammed back into the side of the boat again.

"Too much slack!" Spader cried. "The ropes are getting tangled."

Wham! He hit the side of the ship again.

Could he keep fighting the storm to make it back on board? Or was he going to be pounded senseless first?

EIGHT

Spader spun himself a few times, then faced the hull. This shortened the harness straps, giving them a lot less play and allowing him to control it better.

"Let me try something," Spader yelled to Clayton. He slipped underwater. He needed to stay out of the raging wind. If he could just keep hold of the grips, he might be able to get to the ladder and try climbing again with less slack. He pulled himself along the side of the boat until he was at the ladder.

He rode out another wave, clinging to the hull. The moment it began to recede, he clambered up the ladder. Clayton grabbed his shoulder straps and helped him up and over the rail and onto the deck.

"You all right?" Clayton asked.

"In one piece," Spader said.

"Man overboard!" someone cried.

"Get out the rescue lines," Clayton instructed Spader, who quickly unbuckled his harness.

"On it!" Spader raced to one of the units where the

lines were kept. Someone stood there struggling with the latches.

"Here to help," Spader said.

The worker turned around. "I can do it," Per Watsu snarled.

Spader took a step back. "Yeah? Then why are the lines still in there, instead of out here where they can do some good?"

"I said, I've got it." Per turned his back on Spader and went back to trying to get the hold open.

Spader shoved Per aside. "I can do it faster."

"Spader. Get below. Now."

Spader turned to find Clayton glaring at him.

"But—" Spader protested.

"You're more harmful than helpful up here. If you two can't work together, you're useless."

Spader's cheeks burned with humiliation. He hated being called out like this. And it killed him that Clayton seemed to think he was the one to blame.

"To the engineering level," Clayton snapped. "Now. "

Spader hurried down two levels, his blood boiling. He had done it again. Let Per Watsu get to him.

It was a busy scene on this level too. Water filled the area knee high, and two crew members worked to bring the water pressure back in line.

"What can I do?" Spader asked the nearest crew member. Maybe no one would realize he had been sent down below as a reprimand. At least for now.

"Help Jofels with the connector tubes!" the crew member replied. "The regulators couldn't handle the sudden influx of water!"

Spader joined Jofels, who was pounding a large pipe back into place in the ceiling. By the time they got the pipe back together, Spader noticed that the deck wasn't bucking like a crazed spinney fish anymore.

"I think the storm is losing power," Jofels said. "We're good here, Spader, so go check back in with Clayton."

Rain still came down in sheets, but the wind had calmed and so had the waves. Even so, visibility was nil, and Spader's muscles still ached from the pounding they'd taken while he was being batted around by the roiling waves. He hoped this battle with the elements would be over soon. But he hurried over to Clayton, eager to prove himself.

"Jofels sent me up," Spader said, wanting to be clear that he wasn't disobeying Clayton's instructions.

"Check levels on the upper equalizers," Clayton instructed. "See how close we are to getting back online."

Like all ships on Cloral, the vessel was powered by carefully calibrated water pressure. "Got it." Spader hurried to the nearest gauge. It was off, but was clearly dropping back to a normal level. They didn't want the pressure to drop too quickly, or it could cause an implosion. But the reading wasn't in the danger area. He made his way carefully across the slippery deck to the next gauge.

A thick fog made it impossible to see much farther than a few feet. Spader wondered how far off course they were, and if there were any serious damage.

Clayton came up beside him. "Well, we're not in danger of capsizing or sinking anymore. But until we've reached full equalization, we're not going to be moving."

"Makes sense."

"Go up to the pilot's tower. With some of the systems still offline and this fog, they'll need help navigating."

Spader climbed up the ladder to reach the pilot's tower, where the navigation systems were. "I'm your extra eyes," he told the pilot and the navigator. He placed himself in the forward windows and stared out into the gloom.

"The engineers called up and said the lights should be working any minute now. That will help," the pilot said.

As promised, the lights at the bow of the ship came on.

Spader blinked. "Where did *that* come from?"

Not too far off starboard was another vessel, barely visible in the fog.

"It looks disabled," the navigator said. "See how it's drifting?"

"Probably damaged in the storm," the pilot commented.

"It looks as if it's heading straight toward us!" Spader said.

"They might not be able to steer properly," the navigator said. "It's up to us to keep out of the way."

"Until we do a thorough check, we can't rely on the navigational systems," the pilot said. "Spader, call out instructions based on what you're seeing, while we monitor the instruments as backup. We should be able to get safely past."

There didn't seem to be any signs of life on the disabled vessel. All lights were out, and it just floated steadily toward them. Suddenly there was a loud *boom,* and the window to the pilothouse shattered. Glass and water spewed everywhere.

The pilot keeled over and landed on the floor beside Spader.

Dead.

Nine

"Take cover!" Spader shouted to the navigator. "Raiders go for the pilot's crew first!"

He hit the deck as another blast ripped through the pilot's tower. He rolled quickly across the wet floor just as the navigator thudded down beside him. A quick glance told him the navigator was also dead.

He peered over the instrument board. The raider ship was much smaller than the vessel he was on. That should mean fewer raiders than crew members. Would the crew be able to fend them off?

Only if we have enough weapons. Spader tried to remember from his orientation. Most dangers they faced traveling between habitats were natural—like the storm they had just weathered. Raider attacks were actually pretty rare.

"Stand down!" a voice boomed over the loudspeaker. It sounded like Clayton. "We have a larger crew and weapons to match. And we aren't carrying anything of value."

Spader held his breath. Would the bluff be enough?

"We'll see about that!" a voice challenged from the raider vessel. "Our ship was damaged in the storm. Why should we bother repairing it when you've got a perfectly good one for us to take!"

"Our ship was damaged as well," Clayton said.

Spader knew Clayton must have been stalling for time while the crew either got the ship under way or found a way to attack the raiders. Then he realized—the only way to get the ship moving was from the pilot's tower. His crew didn't know both the pilot and the navigator were dead.

A nasty laugh came over the raiders' system. "You proved it's perfectly seaworthy when you maneuvered out of our way."

It was a trap, Spader thought. *And we fell right into it.*

Usually the raiders kept everyone under guard while they off-loaded whatever cargo they wanted. This time they wanted the ship itself—and they wouldn't want any passengers along. That meant everyone on board would either escape or die.

Spader knew which category he wanted to be in.

Another *boom* rocked the boat. *The raiders must have water canons*, Spader realized. Only water missiles could do such serious damage.

The speakers crackled, and Spader heard a crash as something toppled to the deck.

He crawled to the instrument panel. The raiders probably figured they had taken out the pilot and navigator since the ship wasn't moving. They didn't know that there was one more person still in the tower— and Spader intended to keep it that way.

He pushed out of his mind the sounds of splashes and the exchange of water bullets, screams, and shouts. He had to stay focused. He didn't know the panel well enough to work it blind from the floor, so he pulled himself up into a crouch, keeping his head low.

He peered over the board. Several skimmers and a life raft bobbed on the water, making good speed. One of the jobs of the aquaneers was to ensure the safety of the passengers. Spader figured the personnel from Crasker were in the raft, with aquaneers on the skimmers guiding them. The rest of the crew would defend the ship.

It was up to him to get them out of there.

Sounds on the ladder to the pilot's tower sent Spader into high alert. He darted across the tower cabin and flattened himself against the wall next to the door.

A raider stepped through the doorway, and Spader flung himself at the raider's knees, knocking him off balance. The raider's sleek, silver pistol clattered to the ground, and the raider tumbled down beside it.

Spader leaped onto the raider, never giving him the chance to get back up to his feet. He straddled him and pinned his arms.

The raider squirmed, struggling to flip Spader off. Spader held on and slammed the raider's head onto the floor. He saw the raider's eyes roll up and then shut. The man's body went limp.

Spader stared down at the raider. He had never knocked anyone out before. It felt . . . odd.

He rummaged in the small storage compartment under the navigation board and pulled out some cable. He wrapped it around the raider's wrists and then around the handle of the door. Anything to slow the raider down once he woke up. For good measure he crumpled a navigation chart and stuffed it into the raider's mouth. "No shouting for help for you," Spader told the unconscious man.

That was when he realized—it was quiet. The storm was over and so was the battle down below.

His heart thudded. Had his crew beaten back the raiders?

Keeping his head down, he crept to the navigation board. He just cleared it to peer out the shattered forward windows.

Laughter from below floated up to the tower. But whose? He lifted slightly higher, trying to see down into the hold below.

A head appeared, coming up the stairs on deck.

A raider.

Spader ducked back down.

He swallowed hard and forced himself to look again. His eyes widened. There were two raiders on deck, carrying a dead crew member between them.

"One, two, three!" one of the raiders shouted. Together the two men flung the crew member overboard.

Spader's hands clenched into fists.

"That's the last of 'em," one of the raiders said.

Spader sank back on his heels. The dead pilot and navigator stared up at the ceiling. "What should I do?" he asked them.

The longer he looked at the pilot and navigator, the angrier he became. *Yes.* He would take out the marauding raiders and make them pay for—

He shut his eyes. *No. Think*.

He rubbed his face. What would his father tell him to do? Don't rush to action without knowing the situation. Well, the situation was about as bad as it could get. He was probably the only person left on board from the original crew. Alive, that is.

Benn Spader would tell him to stay that way.

Gradually a plan began to take hold. Energy surged through him. He could do this. He'd need a water sled and an air globe. Yes . . . it was all falling into place.

Of course, first he had to make it out of the tower and get to the storage units two decks below.

He picked up the raider's pistol. He wasn't sure how to use it, but wanted it all the same. His trusty knife was still in his boot.

He peeked over the navigation board again, raising up a little higher so he would get a better view of the entire deck. One of the raiders was relaxed against the rail, while another was helping a raider up the ladder from the water. They seemed to be the only raiders on deck. The others must all have been below. His stomach clenched when he saw Clayton splayed under the struts that had held the loudspeaker. Blood pooled around him from the wounds he'd received. Spader forced himself to look away.

He crawled to the other window, which gave him a view of the back end of the ship. Empty—other than three dead crew members and one dead raider.

There were stairs leading down from the deck to the lower levels both fore and aft. Once he was below, he'd have to hurry past the living quarters and down to where the equipment was stored without being seen.

The first obstacle, though, was getting to the deck. The stairs down from the tower were on the side of the pilothouse. Would he be visible to the raiders at the front of the ship?

He peeked out the back window again. He was about thirty feet above the deck. Was there a way to get down there without using the stairs?

Ducking down again, he searched the cabin for something to use to rappel down the side of the tower. He grabbed more of the cable he had used to tie up the raider. Working quickly, he wrapped the cable several times around the legs of the desk and tied it securely. Then he dropped the line out the window.

He hopped on to the desk, swiveled, then lowered himself out the window. He gripped the cable and winced. "Hobey, that's sharp!" Well, as long as it didn't actually cut him, he'd survive. What was a bit of cable burn compared to being shot by raiders!

Right quick, now, he told himself. He pushed away from the side of the tower and slid down the cable, stopping to swing back into the wall and push off again to take some of the pressure off his hands. His feet touched down. Made it!

He raced across the deck and lay flat at the opening to the cabin level below. He listened intently, straining to hear any sounds of the raiders. He could hear shouts and laughter, but they seemed far away.

He hurried silently down the rungs of the ladder leading below to the living quarters. Good thing no one was around. He was sure they'd hear his ragged breathing and pounding heart.

Spader wondered how many raiders there were. The small vessel they'd abandoned was meant to carry only five or six, but it certainly sounded like there were more of them. And to take out ten experienced crew members, they had to have been pretty evenly matched.

Voices. Coming toward the stairs.

Gotta hide! But where?

There were cabins on either side of the corridor. He didn't want one of those—the raiders would search them carefully for valuables.

He quickly slipped inside one of the nearby supply closets and shut the door.

The shelves of linens had fallen during the storm, and linens were strewn all over the floor. Boxes of toiletries had tumbled over, and a few had popped open. He sat on one of the boxes and let out a shaky breath.

He knew he didn't have long. The supply closets would be checked too.

Something caught his eye. Was it his imagination? It looked as if the pile of linens moved.

He pulled the pistol he'd taken from the raider out of his waistband. He crept to the pile of linen, his heart pounding. Could he actually shoot a raider up close like this?

In a quick move he yanked up the sheet and aimed the weapon.

Straight at Per Watsu.

Ten

"Hobey, mate, you scared me!" Spader blurted out. Then he clapped a hand over his mouth.

Per stared at him, his face whiter than the sheet he was hiding under.

"Guess I scared you too," Spader whispered.

"Is there—is there anyone left?" Per asked.

"I think it's just us," Spader replied, still keeping his voice down. "Do you have any idea how many raiders there are?"

Per shook his head. "When I heard the shots, I didn't understand what was happening. I—I hid."

"Big surprise," Spader muttered.

"I don't see you out there fighting off the raiders," Per snapped.

"I was—oh, shut up," Spader said. "We don't want them to hear us."

"We have to get out of here," Per said.

"State the obvious," Spader said.

Per shot Spader a dirty look. "Do you want to take

shots at me, or do you want to try to get out of here? We may not like this, but we're all we've got. So we should probably try to work together."

Spader hated admitting it, but Per was right. "Sorry," he muttered.

Per pretended to be shocked. "The great Spader is apologizing? You mean you actually admit you're wrong about something?"

"Now who's taking shots?" Spader said. "Why are you always on me? I've never done anything to you."

"Except beat me in every class, test, and competition!" Per blurted out. "It's humiliating."

Spader gaped at Per. "I wasn't trying to make you look bad," he said. "But I'm not going to be sorry for being good."

Per let out a long sigh and looked away. "That's what makes it even worse," he said softly. "You don't even have to try. At the academy I worked so hard to keep up. I sweated for every single grade. Put in extra practice time. You just coasted your way to being everyone's favorite."

Spader didn't know how to respond, so instead he focused on the current problem. "Listen. I have a plan. We get to the raider's disabled vessel and hide out until the raiders leave the area."

"And sit there until we sink like Faar?" Per asked.

"You have a better idea?" Spader demanded.

"The sleds are on the lower level," Per pointed out. "Where most of the raiders are."

"Did you do the sled drill?" Spader asked.

"No," Per admitted. He scowled. "I guess you're

ahead of me. As usual." He gave a hollow laugh. "I can just hear what my father would say about that!"

"Well, your father's not here. So let's stay on the subject," Spader said.

Per slumped but nodded.

"Okay. We know the sleds can be accessed from the water," Spader said. "So we just need to get off the ship, swim to the hatches, and then sled over to the raider ship."

Per looked at him as if he were crazy. "We'll be shot before we hit the waves."

Spader threw up his hands. "Come with me or don't. Because I'm not staying here one minute longer!"

Spader pressed his ear against the door. It had grown quiet again. He pictured his route. Air globes were kept in strategic spots along the corridor. That would be the easy part. Getting into the water would be tougher. He could either dive from the deck above or go down another level to the swim exit.

He cracked open the door. He could still hear laughing and talking down in the cargo area.

Deck it is, he decided.

"Hang on," Per whispered. "I'm going with you."

Spader glanced back at Per. He seemed to have pulled himself together. Spader nodded. "Once we're underwater, follow me to the hatch. I know how to open it."

Spader slipped out of the closet and hurried along the corridor. He grabbed one of the globes hanging near the ladder. He put it on as he clambered up the ladder and peered over the lip of the deck. All clear.

He climbed up to the deck and dashed toward the ladder.

Suddenly an alarm went off, and lights went on in the pilot's tower. Had he been discovered?

No, he realized. They'd found the unconscious raider!

Spader couldn't take the time to be careful. The deck would be swarming with raiders any moment now. He flung himself overboard, cutting into the water clean as a knife.

He kicked hard, wanting to get to the hatches fast. He opened the latch as he had during the drill and pulled out two sleds. Where was Per? Had he changed his mind?

Spader tread water, his heart sinking with each passing moment. No matter how much he tried to push the thought aside, the only conclusion he could reach was that Per had been caught by the raiders.

Now the question was, what should Spader do about it?

ELEVEN

Spader couldn't just leave him. Per was a right dunderhead, and Spader's life would be smooth waters without him, but he couldn't live with himself if he didn't at least try to find out whether the soaker was still alive.

Maybe Per never left that linen closet. That would be where Spader would look first.

Spader poked his head above the ladder and scanned the deck.

Now that the sun had gone down, the deck lights were on, so Spader had no trouble seeing that there were still no raiders at the back end of the boat. But he'd also be spotted immediately if anyone looked.

Spader raced across the deck and dropped onto the ladder leading below. No point even in checking for raiders—they were either there or they weren't.

Luck was with him. The corridor was empty. He pulled the pistol from his waistband again. Now he moved slowly, quietly, deliberately. He listened at each closed door, hoping he'd get some clue to what happened to Per.

He arrived at the linen closet. That door was wide open.

Spader slowed his breathing to calm himself. Then he stepped into the doorway, weapon aimed chest high.

It was empty.

The closet had been his best guess. *Only* guess, truth be told. If Per wasn't in here, Spader would have to search the entire ship, room by room, until he either found him or found his dead body.

He continued along the corridor, stopping and listening at each door. As he approached the last door, he heard talking.

"How many others?" a hard voice demanded. "Where are they hiding?"

"There are no others. How many times do I have to tell you that?"

Spader's heart sped up. Per!

The sound of fist hitting flesh made Spader cringe.

"Let's try this again," the hard voice snarled. "Finding you in that hold was a big surprise. And we don't like surprises."

Per must have heard the raiders coming and found a new hiding place, Spader thought.

"I don't know what you want me to say," Per said, the terror in his voice clear. "I told you the truth and you don't believe me."

"What do you think, Shax?" the hard voice said. "Do you believe him?"

"Keep working on him, Frey." Shax's voice was right on the other side of the door. "Either we'll get the truth out of him, or we'll kill him. Either way we get what we want."

Spader pushed the door in with a quick, powerful flick, slamming it into the raider called "Shax," startling him and knocking him to the floor. Spader jumped into the room and pressed his foot hard onto Shax's neck. He aimed his silver pistol at the raider who had hit Per. Shax grabbed Spader's ankle, but Spader just pressed down harder, cutting off the man's air.

"Wouldn't suggest that," Spader said. "A crushed windpipe is tough to get over."

Shax stopped struggling and Spader eased up. A tiny bit.

"I see why you don't like surprises," Spader said. Without lowering his pistol, he knelt down and disarmed Shax. Now he aimed a weapon at each raider. "They do put you at a disadvantage."

Frey smiled slowly at Spader. "So you got the best of us. But do you really think you can fight off all of us?"

"What I think is that if you leave this guy's not-so-pretty face intact," Spader said, "you can do a lot better than if you leave him for dead."

"Yeah?" Frey smirked. "What makes you think that?"

Spader smiled cheerfully. "I've got a proposition for you."

TWELVE

You slusk fish!" Per exclaimed. "Djungu bug! You hate me so much that you'd side with them?"

Spader just kept smiling. Per's outburst only helped.

"Do you know who this is?" Spader said. "He's Per Watsu. Of Watsu shipyards."

"I can't believe you're doing this to me," Per said.

"You kill him, and what do you have?" Spader continued. "A dead body to unload. But you keep him alive, you have something valuable to sell. I'd bet his daddy would pay a lot of money to get him back in one piece."

"And we get caught making the exchange?" Frey said. "No thank you."

"You're missing the beauty part, mate," Spader said. "Me."

Frey raised an eyebrow. "Yeah? What makes you so beautiful?"

Spader laughed. "I hear I get my good looks from my mother, but what matters is that I can help you pull this off."

"How exactly would you do that?" Frey asked.

"Bring the ship back to Crasker. If I'm the contact from the Grallion vessel, its arrival won't arouse suspicion. After all, I'm on the official list of crew. I can easily make contact with Watsu. That will delay the authorities getting involved. And Daddy Watsu will trust me. He'll think I only have Per's safety in mind."

Spader could tell Frey was thinking it over. "And why would you do us such a favor?" Frey asked. "We killed all your mates."

Spader forced himself not to react, though he seethed inside. "I thought it would be fun to be an aquaneer. But there are too many rules. I'd rather be a raider."

"You never could handle real work," Per spat. "It's always a game to you. I knew this was how you'd turn out all along."

Spader strode across the room and slapped Per across the face. Then he whirled to train his pistol on the raiders again. "See why I want to help you?" he told Frey. "This guy has been a spinney-fish needle in my side through all of my time at the academy."

Frey gave Spader a long, thoughtful look. "Okay," he said finally. "This could work."

"You do understand if we don't trust you," a voice said from the doorway.

Spader turned and saw four raiders, each with a sleek speargun trained on him.

"You're not going to shoot me," Spader said, hoping he was right. "You need me."

"True," Frey said. "For now." He deftly knocked a

pistol out of Spader's hand and kicked it toward Shax. Shax grabbed it, and he, too, aimed it at Spader.

"You know anything about the navigational systems?" Frey asked Spader as he took Spader's other gun. Spader knew there was no point in shooting—not with all those raiders in the doorway.

Spader shook his head. "I'm a junior," he said.

"You mean with your fancy training at the academy you never learned how to pilot one of these?" Shax asked.

Spader shrugged. "I was at the bottom of my class." He saw Per's mouth drop open. Uh-oh. Spader nodded toward Per. "So was he. But I'm slippery good in the water. I'd come in handy if you let me join you."

"Maybe you would, maybe you wouldn't," Frey said. "For now we want you out of our way until we need you." He quickly tied Spader's wrists to the built-in shelving unit. "We'll worry about the systems in the morning. There's got to be manuals up in the tower."

The raiders obviously didn't know this particular vessel's engineering. That meant they wouldn't be under way anytime soon, giving Spader and Per a shot at the original plan to get to the other ship.

The raiders left the cabin, shut the door, and locked it.

"You slimy, low traitor," Per said. "I knew you were no good."

"Shut up, Watsu," Spader snapped. "We have to think fast. Before they get the ship running again."

"Are you crazy?" Per said. "I'm not—"

"Think about it. I was free and clear. But I came back. To rescue your ungrateful hide."

Per stared at Spader. Gradually a look of comprehension came into his eyes.

"Got it now, smart boy?" Spader asked sarcastically. "Thank me later. Now we've got to work on getting free."

Spader strained against the cords that held him. He had just what he needed in his boot, but he didn't think he could reach it. He lifted his leg and bent down as far as he could, hoping he could grab his knife between his teeth, but no go.

"Do you think you can wiggle that seat over here?" Spader said.

"I can try." Per wiggled on the chair, tipping forward and then back. He managed to jerk and wriggle his way across the room.

Spader held up his leg. "My trusty is in my boot."

Per frowned. "Do you want me to get it out with my teeth?"

Spader looked down at Per. "I guess you'll have to turn around."

Per hopped the chair around till his back was to Spader. Spader lifted his foot and placed it where Per could reach it. "Okay, slip your hand in and feel for the knife. But I warn you—I'm ticklish!"

Per pulled the knife from Spader's boot. But there was a new problem. "How do we cut through the cords? Your hands are up too high, and mine are down too low—and both of us would have to do it blind."

"I think if you can get the knife into my hands," Spader said, "I can cut my own cords."

Per stood as best he could, hunched over, with

the chair sticking out from his rear. If their situation weren't so dire, Spader would have laughed.

Spader twisted and slid down as low as possible. "Lean over more," Spader instructed. His fingers felt the blade. "One more inch," Spader said. That did the trick. He grabbed the knife.

"Whoa!" Per tipped over and landed with a clatter on the floor.

Both boys froze.

After a few moments, Spader let out a breath. No one was coming.

"I guess I leaned over too far," Per said, lying sideways on the ground.

"The important thing is that it did the trick." Spader worked on the cords. It was awkward sawing the knife back and forth with his hands tied and without being able to see what he was doing. But he finally frayed the cords enough to pull them apart.

"Free!" he declared.

"Get me up from here," Per said from the floor.

Spader cut through Per's restraints and pulled the chair away as Per stood up.

Spader tried the door. It was locked from the outside. No surprise there. "We need to find another way out."

Per didn't respond.

"You met the crew from Crasker. Do you know whose cabin this was?" Spader asked. "There might be something in the luggage that can help us."

Per just stared off into space. He looked sick.

"Hobey, mate," Spader declared. "We have this one shot at getting out of here. So snap out of it."

Per nodded several times as if Spader's words were slowly making their way into his brain. "We may be able to get into the connector tubes."

"The what?"

"There are tubes that run between all the decks. Some carry air, some carry water. Some do both. They run the systems, including stabilizing and powering. They all connect, that's why they're called connector tubes."

"And you think we can use them to get out?" Spader asked.

"They're big enough to crawl through, in case they need to be repaired," Per said. "If the raiders aren't going online until the morning, then we should be pretty safe."

"How do they work?" Spader asked.

"Little doors raise and lower to let in or stop air and water, shutting off connections or opening them," Per explained. "Sometimes it's done automatically; sometimes by the connections controller crewman down in engineering."

Spader was impressed. Per was actually going to be useful after all. "So how do we find them, and more important, how do we get into them?"

"You search the cabin for anything helpful," Per suggested. "I'll try to find the openings for the connectors. There should be one in this cabin because we're at the spot where the corridor splits. Every change of direction has entry points."

They got to work. Spader pulled open drawers and bags. He dropped to the floor and discovered a small case under the bed. He pulled it out and found a manual, a flashlight, and what looked like a minilocator on a strap: a tiny version of the locating device used on the navigation board. He slipped it onto his wrist.

"I found the connector, but I'm not sure how to get it open," Per said.

Spader joined Per in the closet. Per pointed above them. "There's a cross-section there." Then he pointed to the floor. "And there. So the question is, do we go up or do we go down?"

"Up would take us to the deck. So I say down."

"One thing," Per warned. "We don't know what systems are still online. Or which they'll get working again. If we're in the tubes when the systems go on full power, we could get trapped. Or drown."

"Then we should hurry," Spader said. He looked at the joint where the connector tubes came together. "This is what I helped Jofels repair during the storm."

Spader remembered that the trick had been to push and turn the valves simultaneously. It came open easily.

He and Per stared down into the dark tube. Per was right—it was just big enough to crawl through.

Spader grabbed the flashlight. "Here we go." He lowered himself into the tube.

"I know this ship better than you do," Per protested, dropping down after Spader. "I should lead."

"There's no room in here to change position," Spader argued. "Quit gobbing."

The bottom of the tube was wet, telling Spader that this tube had carried water that powered the systems.

"We should head down to the next level at the first

opportunity," Per said. "We don't want to overshoot the storage units."

"We haven't gone far enough," Spader said. He slid the door over the vertical tube and crawled over it.

He heard Per grumble behind him, but Spader kept going.

They came to a dead end. The only directions to go in were up or down. No more horizontals.

"I told you we'd overshoot," Per said. "We're at the outer connector."

"Where does this one lead?" Spader asked. He really should have let Per lead. Per had already proven he knew a lot more about the way the ship was constructed. It dawned on Spader that just because he didn't like Per didn't mean he shouldn't listen to him. From now on, he vowed, he'd at least *consider* Per's suggestions.

"We're at the outer shell of the ship. We won't be able to access anything from here. It will lead to the hatch that opens directly to the water, to allow it in and out."

Suddenly the unmistakable sound of the ship coming back online made Spader's body tense.

"Oh no!" Per gasped. "The systems are warming up. Any minute now, the water is going to start rushing around these pipes."

"No time to head back," Spader said, sounding calmer than he felt. "We've just got to get to the hatch and out into the water."

Spader lowered himself into the vertical tube. By pressing his back against one side and his feet against the other he was able to walk-slide down the tube. His foot scraped against something in the wall.

The hatch leading outside!

Spader took in a deep breath, then popped open the hatch. They were in luck! This hatch was above the waterline! He remembered from training that depending on load, the vessels sat higher or lower on the water, so there were hatches accommodating the changing equalization.

"We're okay!" he called up to Per. "We're above the water!"

Spader dropped out of the hatch, twisting midair and diving neatly into the water.

Per splashed into the water nearby.

Spader gazed up at the ship. Water poured out of the hatch. "We got out just in time," he said.

"Save your breath," Per said. "We have a ways to go. Without globes or sleds."

Spader guessed the distance between the two vessels was about twice the length of the training canal at the academy. Tough, but possible.

The water was cold and rough. Spader took long, even strokes, wanting to move cleanly through the waves, needing to conserve energy for the distance he'd have to cover. His body gradually warmed up with the exertion, making the water temperature more bearable.

The sky was changing. At dawn they'd become more visible. All Spader could do was swim harder and faster and hope that the raiders weren't looking for them. Yet.

The disabled raider's vessel was growing larger; they were almost there. *Just a few more strokes, a few more kicks.* Spader repeated those words in his head over and over and over. Every muscle in Spader's body felt like rubber. He was having trouble coordinating his legs with his arms, his arms with his breathing. But finally, *finally,* Spader's water-wrinkled fingers touched the hull.

Spader scrambled up the ladder. He was just too tired to swim around to the other side. He knew he'd be fully visible to the raiders, but he didn't care.

Per climbed up right behind him. They lay panting on the deck.

"We made it," Spader murmured. He shut his eyes and felt the deck supporting him.

"Th-That was tough," Per said, his breath coming in gasps.

Spader knew they should try to get the ship up and running. He knew they should go below, where they wouldn't be seen once the sun had risen completely, before the raiders discovered they had escaped. He knew all that, but his body just wasn't going to cooperate. Not yet.

"I—I guess we should check out the instruments," Per said.

Spader groaned. "Hobey, mate. Let's honor this moment. We survived. The plan worked."

"But it's not over yet," Per pointed out.

"You really do know how to bring a fella down, don'tcha?" Spader rolled over and pushed himself up. "All right. Time to get back to the plan."

"Which is what, exactly?" Per asked.

"Wait them out. They get our previous vessel back online while we secretly get this one working again. Then they sail off to the horizon, and we sail off in the exact opposite direction."

"And what if we can't get this vessel working?"

Spader frowned. That was a puzzler.

Per's expression suddenly brightened. "Windworks! This is the exact same ship as the one we worked on when we were assigned alt-power maintenance."

Spader nodded. "Could work. It will take a lot longer to get anywhere, but at least we've got a plan."

He pulled himself to his feet, then immediately ducked back down. "Now we have to come up with Plan B."

"Why?" Per asked, his eyes widening.

"Because we've got raiders heading straight here on water skimmers."

Thirteen

They're coming after us!" Per said.

"Maybe . . . ," Spader said. "They could just be coming over here to pick up supplies."

"Either way," Per said, "it's a real tum-tigger."

"We'll have to fight them off," Spader said.

"With what weapons?" Per asked. "They probably took them all with them. Maybe we can get under way and outrun them."

"On alt power? Are you crazy?"

Now it was Per's turn to demand, "You have a better idea?"

Spader opened and then shut his mouth. He had promised himself to listen to Per. Certainly on anything regarding the ship's inner workings.

"Our chances of surviving are a lot better if they don't get aboard," Per added. "You with me on this?"

"I'm with you." They dashed to the center of the deck and popped open the hatch where the mainmast was stored. Spader locked eyes with Per and gave a sharp nod. "Now!"

They hoisted the mast. Spader knew the moment it was vertical they'd become targets. He just had to hope they could get out of range quickly.

If Per and I die, then the raiders win, Spader thought. *I won't let that happen.*

He flashed mentally to the image of the dead pilot. The dead navigator. Clayton. Fury sent energy coursing through his veins, made his exhausted, depleted muscles push harder. The mast snapped into place.

"I'll tether this," Spader said. "You get the other hatch open."

Per raced to the other hatch while Spader ran the sail up the stand, then raced to the back of the boat and tied it off. The sail ballooned out, catching the strong wind. *This might work! Good for Per!*

Boom! The window in the pilot's tower shattered.

"They've seen us!" Per cried.

"Keep at it!" Spader ordered.

Spader hurried to the rail, staying low. He had to tie off another line to secure the sails on the mainmast. He lashed the line to the cleat, then risked a look across the water. The raiders were getting closer. His eyes raised to the vessel, and his heart jumped into his throat.

A line of raiders stood at the rail of the Grallion transport ship, each of them armed. Worse, there was a raider on the ship's deck manning a small water cannon, designed to deliver the deadly, powerful water missiles.

"Faster!" Spader yelled. He dashed to the bow, where Per struggled to raise the foresail. With only the mast sails raised, the vessel wouldn't be stable. They'd tip with each wave and every gust of wind.

"We've got to get balanced!" Spader said, clutching the strut holding the bottom of the sail.

"I know!" Per cried.

Spader heard a shrill whine. He pushed Per's head down. "Duck!"

Another missile slammed into the tower, shattering glass and spurting water.

"They must think we've got a pilot up in the tower. They're following their usual pattern," Spader said. "That could help us. It'll keep 'em busy."

Per worked the pulley system that raised the sail. Done! The two sails were in place.

Boom! A water missile hit the front sail, ripping a hole right through it, spraying the deck with water. The force caused the line to release from the tip of the bowsprit—the pole that stuck out over the water from the bow. Spader grabbed the line before it unhitched completely.

"They're targeting the sails!" Per shouted above the wind.

"I can see that. But we're moving!"

"We've got to get that front sail back in place," Per called.

"I'm on it. You work the main sail."

Per crawled to the center of the vessel as Spader crawled along the bowsprit. He could hear the sound of rapid fire. The raiders had stopped launching water missiles and were using their rifles and handheld launchers.

Spader took the line in his teeth and clung with his hands and knees to the long shaky pole. He inched out over the rough water, feeling the spray in his face. The ship was moving, which was great, but the waters were choppy, and until they were stabilized, the ship could tip over. Getting equilibrium without the usual systems was touch-and-go under the best of circumstances, Spader knew. Trying to do it while under fire, well, this was new territory.

Spader felt the breeze of water bullets whizzing by just above his head. He kept going. He had to tie off this line.

He made it to the cleat. Wrapping one arm tightly around the bowsprit and pressing his legs hard into it, he took the line from his mouth and lashed it into place.

"Yah!" Spader yelped. Searing pain in his shoulder knocked him off the pole. Just before he hit the water, he grabbed the bowsprit with his good hand and dangled over the surface.

He swung his legs, working to get momentum, and kicked up hard. He grabbed the bowsprit with his legs and hooked the elbow of his good arm over the pole. He hung there, with his back to the water, belly to the bowsprit, knees wrapped over the pole. A total target.

But the ship had stabilized. Per must have gotten the main worked out, and now the fore was in place as well.

If he could just stay alive long enough to get back on the ship.

"Spader! The skimmers are almost here!" Per cried.

Oh, yeah . . . Spader had forgotten about them.

Spader knew he looked ridiculous, hanging from the bowsprit like a basket and edging backward toward the ship. And it was tougher slithering feet first, under the pole rather than above it, and using only one arm. But he did it.

Back on deck he crouched low. He spotted Per huddled by the rail, working the main sail, keeping his head down.

"You're injured!" Per said as Spader dropped down beside him.

"Am I?" Spader said. He didn't want to admit the pain and loss of blood was making him light-headed.

A head appeared above the rail, midship on the opposite side of the deck.

"Company," Spader whispered.

"Should we hide?" Per asked, the terror in his voice clear.

"Not enough time," Spader said. "Besides, all that will do is delay the inevitable."

"Right. So fight it is."

They both scanned the deck, trying to find weapons.

"To change direction we release this line and the boom swings across the deck, right?" Spader was trying to remember the maneuver they had practiced back on Grallion.

"You think if we altered course, we'd get away faster? But we still have to get rid of these guys!"

"I think it's *how* we can get rid of them. When I holler 'Now,' release the boom."

"What are you—"

"No time to explain, just do it!"

"You got it!"

There were now two raiders on deck. Spader needed to get them in just the right position. And hope Per had lightning fast reflexes. Otherwise Spader would be full of water bullets.

"Here I go!" Spader stood and dashed along the rail. "Hey, mates! Over here!"

The two raiders whirled around toward the sound of his voice. This put them at the perfect angle. . . . "NOW" Spader shouted.

He ducked as the long boom swung across the deck. It connected with the two raiders and knocked them over the rail.

"Whoo-hoo!" Spader cheered.

"We did it!" Per shouted.

Spader shaded his eyes. The distance between them and the other ship had doubled. They weren't completely out of range, but the attack had stopped.

He gazed down at the water. The raiders were skimming back to their ship.

Spader joined Per, who was lashing the main sail into place. "Why are they giving up?" Per asked.

Spader shrugged. "We're not worth the trouble. By the time we get back to Grallion or Crasker, they'll be long gone, and we'll have no idea where they went."

"How will we get back?" Per asked.

Spader grinned and held up his good arm.

"What's that?" Per asked.

"A minilocator," Spader said. "It's one of the new devices the engineers from Crasker were bringing to Grallion."

"Do you know how to use it?" Per asked.

"Not a clue. But I figure between the two of us, I bet we can work it out."

Per smiled. "I bet you're right!"

"That was some sight," Wu Yenza told Per and Spader five days later. "The ship arriving under wind power."

It had taken them four days to return to Grallion, and this had been the first day they had reported for duty. Wu Yenza had surprised them by giving them a half day off, and taking them out to celebrate their safe return. They had just arrived at the entrance to a popular tavern.

"You're taking us to Grolo's?" Spader asked. "That's right spiff!" It was a favorite among the senior staff.

Wu Yenza smiled. "I'd say you two have earned it."

They pushed through the doors and joined a group of other aquaneers, who applauded as Per and Spader walked up to the table.

"If I hadn't seen it with my own eyes, I wouldn't have believed it," Spader's neighbor, Tradco, said.

"Even more remarkable," Wu Yenza said. "These two alone on that ship, and they didn't kill each other!"

Everyone laughed. "We came pretty close," Spader admitted. "But Per really knew his stuff. Knowing the innards of the vessel the way he did gave us a real advantage."

Per gave a small smile. "Thanks, mate. You have some skills as well."

"Okay, now I know I've witnessed a miracle," a supervisor said. "You two complimenting each other?"

"That minilocator you brought back is a real gem," another aquaneer said.

"It did *us* right, that's for sure," Spader said.

"I'll never complain about alt power again," Per added. "In fact, maybe that will become my area of specialty on Prongo."

"Your transfer came through?" Spader asked.

"The notice was in my mail when I got home," Per said.

Spader nodded. "Good for you." He knew how badly Per wanted that posting and how important it was to prove himself to his father. Getting the assignment he wanted would help in that goal. *And not having me around showing him up will probably help too*, Spader mused.

He didn't hate Per anymore, but he was still . . . Per.

The door to the tavern swung open and a tall man walked in. Press!

Spader got up and went to greet him.

"What are you doing here?" Spader asked his father's friend.

"I heard you had yourself quite the adventure," Press said. "I wanted to find out for myself."

"How did you hear?" Spader asked. He hadn't even told his parents yet what had happened.

Press shrugged. "Things get around, if you know how to listen."

"It was pretty unbelievable," Spader said.

"You're right about that," a belligerent voice nearby muttered.

Spader turned and saw a stocky man scowling into his drink.

"Did you say something?" Spader demanded.

"Spader . . . ," Press began.

The man turned to face Spader. "I've been hearing all the tales the last few days. Sorry, I don't buy it."

Spader clenched the fist of his good arm. He stepped closer to the man. "Are you calling me a liar?"

He felt Press's hand on his shoulder. "No, Spader. Don't spoil the celebration by taking the bait."

Spader's jaw worked as he tried to hold back the anger.

Press squeezed Spader's shoulder. "Still have to learn to control those emotions," he murmured, almost so quietly Spader could barely make out the words.

Spader took in a breath and decided to back down. He forced a smile onto his face and said, "Believe what you want, mate. No worries here." He allowed Press to steer him away from the bar and back toward the table.

"Isn't Per the lad you got into a scuffle with at the academy?" Press asked.

"My father told you?" Spader asked.

Press shrugged. "We talk about you a lot," he said.

"Per's not so bad, I guess," Spader said. "I wouldn't want to be him. All that pressure from his father. I guess it's why he can be such a . . ." He struggled to find the right word.

"A djungo bug?"

"Exactly." Spader's brow furrowed. "On board with the raiders I realized, just because he's a djungo bug, doesn't mean he's wrong about everything." He gave a wry smile. "Things might have even gone a little more smoothly if I'd listened to him a bit more."

Press grinned. "That's a big lesson—to respect the knowledge of others even if it comes from someone you don't like." He laughed. "It was hard for me to learn that I didn't know everything when I was your age."

"Press!" Wu Yenza said. "When did you get to Grallion?"

"Just today," Press said. He and Spader settled at the table.

"How long do you plan to stay?" Spader asked.

Press shrugged. "I'm not sure yet. I may have some . . . work."

"How's that arm of yours?" someone asked Spader.

"Doc says I'll be good as new in a few weeks," Spader replied, holding up the sling. "Till then I'll just lie on my hammock and grill Kooloo fish."

"Think again," Wu Yenza said. "There's plenty of other work you can do."

Spader groaned. "Please, I'm already injured. Don't hurt me more."

Wu Yenza smiled. "I know what will ease your pain," she said. "First round of sniggers is on me!"

ℿow you know the stories of Kasha's, Gunny Van Dyke's, and Vo Spader's lives before they met Bobby Pendragon.

Ready for more? Don't miss the next installment of Pendragon: Before the War, available in February 2009, featuring Aja Killian, Elli Winter, and Alder. Read on for a sneak peek at Alder's story. . . .

Alder whirled, caught Neman's elbow with a sharp blow. His blade went flying. But then Eman gave him another whack. That one stung!

As Alder turned his attention to Eman, Neman retrieved his sword. "Lucky shot, you big oaf," Neman said, whacking him in the leg.

Alder began retreating, a sinking feeling running through him. As he backpedaled, trying desperately to keep both Eman and Neman in front of him where he could fend them off, he saw a figure leaning against a nearby tree.

Relief flooded through him. It was Wencil. Good old Wencil would get him out of the jam!

"Wencil!" he called.

Wencil smiled broadly. "You're doing great, boy!" he called.

Doing great? Was Wencil joking?

Alder gave his instructor an imploring look. But the old man just crossed his arms and continued to lean against the tree, a placid smile on his face.

Distracted by Wencil, Alder left himself open and several more blows caught him—one on the shin, one on the arm, and one nasty stinging blow across the face.

Alder realized that he wasn't going to win. That much was completely, painfully obvious. But he realized that if he was going to take a beating, at least he might achieve his goal of helping the Milago boy. If he could do that, then Eman and Neman would still have lost.

Alder reached into his belt, pulled his knife. With a flurry of blows, he managed to drive Eman and Neman back, opening just enough space to allow him to sprint toward the Milago boy. With a quick slash of his knife, he cut the boy free.

"Go!" he hissed.

The boy blinked. "Why did you—"

"Go!" Alder yelled it this time.

The boy didn't have to be told again. He turned and ran like a scared rabbit. And like a rabbit, he escaped by disappearing suddenly into a small hole in the ground.

Alder's focus on freeing the Milago boy, unfortunately, had put him in a bad position. Eman and Neman were now closing in on him from opposite directions. He couldn't fight them off both at once. Not without growing another pair of arms.

He decided it was time for a retreat.

It was then that his oversize body caught up with him. He had never had the steadiest feet in the world. So when his toe snagged on a root, he staggered and went down with a heavy thump.

Eman and Neman leaped forward, slapping him unmercifully with the flats of their swords. He had no option but to curl up in a ball and take it. The blows rained down on him from all sides.

Where is Wencil? he thought bitterly. *When's he finally going to intervene?* But as he snuck a glance at the tree where the old man had been leaning, the last shred of hope leached away. Wencil was gone.

"We'll quit," Eman said, "as soon as you admit we're stronger."

"Just say it, Milago-lover!" Neman added, whacking him hard in the arm. "'I'm a weakling.'"

"Weakling!" Eman said. "Weakling!"

Then a thin, clear voice cut through the air. "Over here, you Bedoowan creeps!"

Alder looked to where the voice was coming from. Now he saw it: The Milago boy's body was poking up from the hole in the earth. He was waving furiously.

"Over here!" the boy called again.

Alder still had his ipo stick gripped in his hand. He desperately swung it in a wide circle. Eman and Neman leaped back to avoid getting whacked in the shins. It gave Alder just enough time to stagger to his feet and start sprinting toward the hole where the Milago boy was.

"That's right!" Eman yelled. "Keep running, you chicken!"

Alder looked over his shoulder. Eman and Neman were trotting after him. Not rushing—but following fast enough that Alder knew he had no choice. Go down the hole or keep getting beaten.

"Follow me!" the Milago boy shouted.

Alder didn't have to think twice. Even though the idea of hiding in some overgrown rabbit hole didn't appeal to him, he couldn't stand the idea of any further humiliation. He dove into the hole. What the hole was, where it led, or why it was there—none of these question entered his mind. All he could think about was escape.

"This way!" the Milago boy whispered. The hole was deeper, larger, darker than Alder expected. Now that he was here, it occurred to him to wonder what kind of hole this was.

"What is this place?" Alder said.

But the Milago boy didn't answer. He simply

disappeared from view, as though he'd fallen through a trapdoor.

Alder felt around blindly in the darkness. His hands closed around the rungs of what was obviously a ladder. So that was where the Milago boy had gone. Down the ladder.

"Weakling! Weakling!" Above him two sword points were probing into the hole. If he just sat there, Alder realized the points would soon be probing holes in his legs.

Without another thought Alder grabbed the ladder and descended into the darkness. After eight or ten rungs, he reached the bottom and found himself in a long tunnel lined with torches. The Milago boy was nowhere to be seen.

It was only then that he realized where he was.

I'm in the mines! he thought. *Now I'm going to die!*

BEFORE BOBBY PENDRAGON . . .

BEFORE SAINT DANE . . .

BEFORE THE WAR

DON'T MISS A SINGLE INSTALLMENT OF

PENDRAGON
BEFORE THE WAR

BOOK ONE OF THE TRAVELERS
On sale in January

BOOK TWO OF THE TRAVELERS
On sale in February

BOOK THREE OF THE TRAVELERS
On sale in March